Aerial Dance

Aerial Dance: A Guide to Dance with Rope and Harness provides an introduction for the beginning aerialist. It covers rigging, equipment, advice on optimal conditioning, and a step-by-step guide to technique, including anatomical references, space and time considerations, and elements of force when working with and against gravity. Specific movements and choreography are framed anatomically and together reflect the pattern and order of an aerial technique class. Challenges inherent to this type of dancing are discussed, as well as wellness instruction and methods of altering these techniques for intermediate and advanced dancing. A companion website hosts video that corresponds with the technique and phrasing in the book.

Jenefer Davies is the Associate Professor of Dance at Washington and Lee University and Artistic Director of the W&L Repertory Dance Company. She received an MFA in Choreography and Performance from The George Washington University, and a MALS in Dance from Hollins University. Her choreography has been commissioned by dance, opera, and theatre companies and has toured to Spain, Greece, Scotland, and throughout the United States. Davies founded the contemporary modern dance company, Progeny Dance, which has performed at Green Space and Dixon Place in Manhattan, and annually at The Center for Performance Research in Brooklyn. Her work has been supported by the Virginia Commission for the Arts; Washington and Lee University's Lenfest Grants, Johnson Fund, and Glenn Grants; the Treakle Foundation; and an Associated Colleges of the South Mellon grant. She created one of the first academic programs in aerial dance in the country and her aerial dancers have performed at the Ailey Citigroup Theatre in NYC, at the Corcoran Gallery of Art in Washington DC, and from the rooftops of buildings on the Washington & Lee campus. Davies has been published in the International Planetarian Magazine, ICHPER-SD World Congress on Dance, the Nu Delta Alpha Journal and the Athens (Greece) Institute for Research in the Arts Consortium. She serves on the Editorial and Reviewer's Board of the Athens Journal of Humanities and Arts and has reviewed dance proposals for Oxford University Press.

Aerial Dance

A Guide to Dance with Rope and Harness

Jenefer Davies

Routledge
Taylor & Francis Group

NEW YORK AND LONDON

First published 2018
by Routledge
711 Third Avenue, New York, NY 10017

and by Routledge
2 Park Square, Milton Park, Abingdon, Oxon OX14 4RN

Routledge is an imprint of the Taylor & Francis Group, an informa business

Library of Congress Cataloging in Publication Data
A catalog record for this title has been requested

ISBN: 978-1-138-69911-3 (hbk)
ISBN: 978-1-138-69899-4 (pbk)
ISBN: 978-1-315-45245-6 (ebk)

Typeset in Times New Roman and Helvetica
by Florence Production Ltd, Stoodleigh, Devon, UK

Visit the companion website: www.routledge.com/cw/davies

For Emma –
who flew high with me in utero
and has been ever since

Contents

Figure A.1 A beautiful smile on the descent

Credit: © Washington and Lee University 2009

Acknowledgments

Erik Jones, Emma Davies-Mansfield, Vanessa Davies and John Paulus, Maggie Davies, Mickey Hartnett and John Kish, and Antony and Kristina Davies. For proof reading the first to the ten thousandth draft. For freely sharing gifts of hugs and gifts of wine and knowing which was needed the most at any given time. For never failing to believe I could do anything. You inspire me. You hold me aloft.

The beautiful and fierce Washington and Lee University and Roanoke Ballet Theatre aerial dance students and performers

The Associated Colleges of the South, Andrew W. Mellon Grant

Athens Institute for Education and Research, Visual and Performing Arts Division

Terry Sendgraff, Joanna Haigood and Amelia Rudolph

Wendy Hesketh, Wired Aerial Theatre and The Higher Space Liverpool

Erik Skinner and Daniel Kirk

Sharon Witting and Andrea Burkholder

Jason Schumacher

Adam Gentry

Michelle Kadikian

Stu Cox and ZFX

Roanoke Ballet Theatre, Ann and Bill Hopkins and Mary Anne Marx

Center in the Square and Dr. James Sears

Stacey Walker, Meredith Darnell, and Kristina Siosyte, Taylor & Francis

At Washington and Lee University:

Mr. and Mrs. H. F. Gerry and Marguerite Lenfest

Elliot Emadian '17, Jennifer Ritter '13, Erin Sullivan '13, Dana Fredericks '12, student researchers and performers

Hank Dobin, Professor of English

Paul Burns, Director of Environmental Health and Safety

Scott Bebee, Director of Energy Initiatives

Kevin Remington, University Photographer

Shawn Paul Evans, Head of the Department of Theatre, Dance and Film Studies

James Dick, Director of Outdoor Education

Tom Hackman, Technical Director, Department of Theatre, Dance and Film Studies

Owen Collins, Professor of Theatre

Marc Connor, Provost

Suzanne Keen, Dean of the College

LeAnne Shank, General Counsel

Chris Schall, Fitness Center Director and Strength and Conditioning Coach

John Lindberg, Manager of Technical Operations, Lenfest Center for the Arts

Jessica Miller, Costumer

Rob Mish, Director, Lenfest Center for the Arts

Susan Wager, Associate Director, Lenfest Center for the Arts

Rena Cromer, Box Office Coordinator

Phil Brulotte, former Technical Director

All photographs taken by Kevin Remington. Copyright 2009–2017 Washington and Lee University. All rights reserved.

Figure A.2 A powerful slice through the air
Credit: © Washington and Lee University 2011

What is Aerial Dance?

Aerial Dance is imbued with grace and the appearance of weightlessness, which creates an ethereal experience. Untethered from the ground, the aerial dancer must possess different sensibilities, both mental and corporeal. This art form requires the performer to possess power, strength of body and mind, the ability to adapt to a new and changing environment, and an inherent understanding of where the body lies in relationship to the space around it. Such adaptation requires a fortitude that is both physically and mentally powerful, yet still responsive. Behind the aerialist's apparent ease while performing must lie a deep and powerful trust in the space, the equipment, and the rig. In the best scenario, the aerialist appears to be a celestial being rather than a body upon which gravity acts. The paradox of this art form is that an immense mental and bodily strength lies underneath the appearance of effortlessness.

The differences between aerial dance and traditional dance forms are many; they include the relationship between the dancer and gravity, the dancer and direction, and the dancer and force. The aerialists' world is literally turned on its side. Traditional concepts of alignment, the force necessary to push away from the wall, distance gained in jumps and leaps, and timing and landing suddenly become uncertain and fluid. Alignment is an internal process of sensing, as opposed to an external use of mirrors. The way that muscles engage, give in to, and resist gravity has shifted 90 degrees. When an aerialist lowers into demi plié, for example, not only is she engaging, among other things, the muscles of the feet, legs, spine, abdominals and gluteals, but these muscles are working while the entire torso is being pressed down upon. In contrast with traditional dance, gravity does not help the aerial dancer's release into plié. Conversely, it is pulling on the perpendicular body. In this way, the psoas must be contracted to keep the legs in a specific place on the wall. The neck is long but engaged as the head works to maintain alignment with the shoulders. As the arms move, they are resisting the pull downward. In short, the body fights the pull of gravity as it works to remain parallel with the ground while also aligned within itself. The challenges in alignment are coupled with a new relationship to the "floor" (traditionally a wall of a building or some other vertical surface). For instance, pushing away from this "floor" generally yields more time aloft than a traditional jump would. Of course, this is in relationship to a dancer's height on the wall and the length of the rope to which they are tethered, so a new force-to-reaction ratio is created. Every time the aerialist's position on the wall changes, so too does the ratio.

Figure 0.1 Aerial dance performance shot that includes dancers, riggers, tech crew, and audience

Credit: © Washington and Lee University 2009

All of these factors necessitate a new relationship between the dancer and time. A dancer knows instinctually how long it takes to land when she jumps from a plié in first position. The dancer's proprioceptors (and rehearsal) have taught her what to expect. Time in aerial dance fluctuates and is a combination of effort, body position, and height on the vertical surface. For example, if a dancer is 40 feet in the air, planked on a vertical surface that is 80 feet tall and she pliés in first position, pushing away, the amount of effort she exerts coupled with the fact that she has 40 feet of rope to play with means that she will fly out at a certain speed over a certain distance. If her body was open in an "X" position, with arms and legs out at 45 degree angles, she may not have as much speed, due to the wind resistance or the positioning of her feet. This could change the speed with which, and potentially the distance, she pushes away from the wall. Or, alternately, if she pushes away in the "X" position with more force then she did while in the planked position, she may end with the same speed and distance as the plank push. Intriguingly, there can be a multitude of variables for any given dancer. It is through experimentation and rehearsal, among other things, that we learn to adapt to these uncertainties.

A fascinating internal reorganization occurs in aerial dance. The dancer can no longer rely on the visual aid of a mirror. There is no visual feedback to pair with our internal dialogue. Learning becomes a combination of internal assessment and verbal response from others.

As the dancers master their new relationship with gravity and receive feedback, the body learns to adjust. For example, hanging upside down with legs extended up the rope and torso dangling from inside the harness, the dancer may feel her body is creating a long line from toe to head. Many times, the reality of the situation is that the lumbar is arched due to the natural push of the harness, the arms are hanging behind the central axis of the body, and the back of the neck is flexed. Through muscular reorientation and instructor response, the dancer learns that alignment in a vertical position may mean pressing the abdominals back against the harness to elongate the lumbar, pressing the shoulders slightly forward from the girdle for engaged arms and looking straight ahead (or in our case, up) to elongate the back of the neck. The effect of gravity on the body is always changing based on positioning, height of the dancer, length of the rope, and movements. It is a constant dialogue, and a new learned pattern of movement behavior.

Aerial dance is a process of fighting against, and working with, gravity over and over again. Gravity becomes your partner and, like a human partner, it is sometimes paired with a powerful force that rocks or spins the dancer. However, it can also serve as a guiding force, a tool in carving space, and a place of relaxation or release. The variations in the shapes of an aerialist's movement, her speed, force, and direction affect gravitational and centrifugal forces that encourage the body to react, produce response and, in so doing, create the next movement (which begins the process again). The cycle becomes a conversation. The conversation between partners is present throughout the dance. It is an intriguing relationship that excites both dancer and audience, as the continuing dialogue unfolds.

C H A P T E R   1

The Rig

CERTIFIED RIGGER

It should be noted quite emphatically here that this book DOES NOT condone, suggest or support anyone rigging for aerial dance who is not a certified, licensed and bonded rigger. There are various types of riggers so it's important that when discussing your needs, you make it very clear that you need someone who is licensed to rig *people*. There are certified riggers who are licensed to rig sets, objects and overhead structures. However, this sort of rigging certification is for static loads. That is, a structure that hangs with no movement. Certified riggers for aerial dance understand load and dynamics. This is especially important

Figure 1.01 Learning the ropes
Credit: © Washington and Lee University 2009

given the fact that aerial dancers move and swing. The load for an aerial dancer isn't just his/her weight. Movement changes and multiplies the load exponentially.

Before hiring someone, don't be embarrassed to ask to see the rigger's ETCP (or other) certification. Individuals who have received certification should have a combination of a degree from an accredited program, internship and apprenticeship hours, and experience in the professional rigging field, and will have passed a comprehensive exam. The ETCP exam covers algebra and geometry and focuses on static, dynamic and shock load, distribution, protection, rigging materials, implementation, operations and management and a variety of rigging systems. If you're looking into a specific rigger and you've never heard of the certification program or the rigging company from which he/she is associated, do your research. There is a ton of information concerning companies and programs in aerial certification online. If you feel overwhelmed by the information, call a professional theatre that you respect who regularly flies actors/dancers and ask their advice. Broadway theatres have standards that they are required to adhere to. Find out what companies they use and what rigging certification companies they respect. Speak with professional aerial dance or circus companies. Do extensive research and ask questions. Your safety is paramount so being positive that your rigger is qualified is essential.

Also of importance before hiring a rigger is securing a copy of their insurance. You should be sure that the person you are employing to rig your studio or show has insurance of at least $1 million, preferably $2 million. This protects them and you and should not be left out of the discussion. A professional rigger will be licensed and bonded, usually, through their certifying association. The person who can best describe the role of a rigger is my friend, colleague and rehearsal rigger, Adam.

Rigging for Aerial Dance, by Adam Gentry

With 13 years in entertainment rigging, Adam has installed and maintained acrobatic rigging systems in over 30 countries. He is a head rigger and flyman through I.A.T.S.E. Local 55 *and is ETCP certified. He is currently on tour with* Aladdin/Disney Theatrical.

As anyone who has any interest in aerial dance knows, one cannot perform aerial dance without being suspended. It seems so simple – attach your ropes to something – make art. But there are so many questions. How is it attached? What is it attached to? Has it been maintained? By whom? When? What kind of anchor? What kind of bolt? Has it ever been overloaded? There are hundreds of types of anchors and hundreds of thousands of people who install them incorrectly. Your needs could be as simple as a single point on the grid, or as complicated as a moving multi line fly system in a theatre or a computer controlled fully automated rigging system that can fly you around the room. For every kind of rig, no matter how small, you need to hire a professional. Guessing that something can hold you is a recipe for disaster. Professional riggers are able to do the math required to know if the hardware is rated for your particular movements in your performance. They will be able to inspect the attachment point, the architecture of the space and the engineering of the ceiling and they will be able to explain to you exactly why it can bear the load of the dance. They will also be able to explain why the piece of hardware you bought at your local home improvement store is not only questionable, it is completely unsafe. Please, take rigging very seriously.

There are dozens of books and endless online resources devoted to rigging in entertainment and arts performances. However, rigging is not something you can do safely after reading a few instructions and looking at pictures on the internet. As a performer, it is you that is ultimately responsible for your own safety and equipment. Although a professional is rigging you, you should know your personal equipment inside and out. You should know what it is, how it works and what to look for concerning wear and tear. Your equipment should be inspected before each and every use. It may seem redundant, but even the smallest bit of damage can become a major problem if left unchecked.

Your safety is YOUR responsibility. Be educated, and always hire a professional to do your rigging. Most accidents are due to something that could have been easily prevented. Attention to detail will not only make for a better show for you and your audience, it may just save your life.

EQUIPMENT

Rigging for aerial dance can involve anything from simple, single point, manual rigs to extremely complex, multi-person, motorized assemblies. Since it's impossible to describe every possible rig incarnation, I will describe here the rig I use which is a model I've honed over many years and feel is a good middle ground between accessibility and cost. The rig is fairly simple with only few moving parts. This is beneficial in a few ways. Because the rig is uncomplicated, with no automated parts or complex machinery, the cost of rigging is quite low. Additionally, the simpler the rig, the fewer moving parts, the safer it is. It lessens the *P&E factor*. This is one of the basic safety considerations I cover with new aerial students on the first day of class. The concept was suggested to me by my friend and colleague James Dick, who is the Director of Outdoor Education at W&L. The P&E factor states that the greatest chance of failure in aerial safety can be attributed to either *People* or *Equipment* (and many times the people can be the cause of the equipment problem). Both of these are preventable with proper care and awareness. In the case of my rig, the simpler the equipment set up, the fewer opportunities for people and/or equipment to fail.

For the sake of organization, I will format the discussion of aerial dance equipment beginning with those elements closest to the dancer and work my way to the farthest aspect of the rig. The order of my set up is: safety helmet, harness, carabiner, grigri, rope, ascender with attached loop, carabiner, swivel, carabiner, gacflex spanset.

Figure 1.02

Aerial performance

Credit: Washington and Lee
University 2009

Safety Helmet

I require all of my students to wear a safety helmet anytime they are on a vertical surface. They hate it and find them *very* unfashionable, but they are essential for aerialists. I found a versatile mountaineering helmet by Petzl that is extremely durable and has many adjustable features. This aids in budgeting as it fits many shapes and sizes of heads, which means I am able to purchase fewer helmets. Because the wall on which we typically rehearse is black, I bought bright red helmets so that it's very obvious if someone has forgotten (or "forgotten") to put it on. This helmet has wheels inside it that adjust the inner size of the hat both front to back and on the sides. The chinstrap is also adjustable and there are a large number of ventilated holes in the top and sides. The holes create a more agreeable environment inside the helmet by allowing for venting of sweat and smells (and encourage less grumbling since the students usually have to share.) It's important that these helmets are aligned properly on the head (I will go into detail about this later in Rigging the System, Safety Helmet, p. 16). I can't stress enough how important these safety helmets are. A few students hit their heads on the cinderblock wall every semester. The use of the helmet keeps the students safe and gives them and me peace of mind. A wonderful advantage of this safety measure is that while protecting them, it also encourages experimentation and the good sort of risk taking.

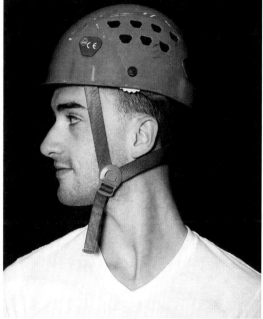

Figure 1.03 Proper helmet placement on the brow
Credit: © Washington and Lee University 2016

Figure 1.04 Proper placement of the side and chin straps
Credit: © Washington and Lee University 2016

Harness

While professional aerial dance companies generally have harnesses specially made for them that suit the specific needs of the dancer and/or choreographer, when teaching aerial in the university classroom, time and cost are large factors. I give up specificity of purpose and cutting edge design in order to stay on budget and have easy access to and fast delivery of equipment. I use climbing harnesses that are available to the general public. This helps to keep the cost down and also, because they are made for climbing, has the added benefit of features that are simple to understand and use and are engineered for safety. Because I never know how many students will be enrolled in my class, I can reuse harnesses for a period of time (see Equipment Care, p. 24) and simply order new ones if necessary for a larger class, and have them within a few days. I have used a variety of harnesses over the years for various reasons. I began aerial dance through a collaboration with climbers so the first harnesses I used were various models from Black Diamond, Misty Mountain and Petzl. I liked these types of harnesses because they allowed for a full range of motion. They didn't restrict backwards or upside down movement and they didn't force me to sit upright or create a break in my lower lumbar when I planked. I felt like I could move my legs freely to some extent (there is always a little bit of leg restriction in harnesses by virtue of their basic design). The harness is very lightweight and breathable.

It doesn't feel like it adds any weight to your body as you move. The rear riser is elastic. This is nice because you aren't restricted when you need a larger, freer movement but you have some stability in maintaining alignment. It's nice too that during rest periods, you can shift the leg loops, due to the elasticity of the riser, and relieve some of the pressure from your upper thighs and pelvis. The waist belt is comfortable. It's not overly padded but there is some padding there to help reduce abrasions to the waist and hips area. At the time I purchased the harnesses, the models did not have double backed legs or waistband. This opened me up to a greater chance of human error. Also, because the legs and waist weren't a closed loop system, the students could easily open them up and sometimes get confused about how the various items were threaded. In the beginning, I never had any need to use the equipment loops (gear loops). At one point I considered removing them because, although I'm very clear during my safety lectures, my fear has always been that new students will mistakenly attempt to harness their carabineer into a gear loop instead of the correct belay loop and injure themselves. However, altering a harness to any degree, even if it appears as though it has no effect, compromises its safety. NEVER mess with your harness. Even what would seem to be the most mundane task like marking your name on a harness with an indelible marker (the chemicals in the ink can potentially damage it and decrease its strength) can harm it. Later, when I began teaching at a university, I looked into harnesses with greater built in safety features. At the front of my mind was the fact that harnesses are not designed to be used for inverting. In fact, given that its purpose is for fall

Figure 1.05 Proper placement of a sit harness
Credit: © Washington and Lee University 2016

arrest, climbing harness manufacturers specifically do not want the person wearing it to go upside down. However, this is an essential part of aerial dance so I tried to find a harness that would allow inverted movement without completely restricting the body and still be completely safe. After much research, I purchased Singing Rock Expert II, which is a very strong, very heavy harness that is used by workers who have to scale high-rise buildings for things like construction or window cleaning. I bought this model because it has a pelvis and chest harness combination, which is detachable and can be sized to suit many body types. The chest harness protects the dancers during inversions and is especially helpful for new aerialists who don't trust the equipment. This, along with the permanently double backed leg loops and waistband, minimized the human risk involved in this type of activity. For some students, this is their first and only exposure to a harness. Assuming every student has no experience with harnesses and purchasing fail-safe models is a good plan. (For more safety policies, see Safety Checklist, p. 23.) One nice feature of the Singing Rock harness is that, apart from the traditional lap clip-in point, it has side and back clip-in points as well. The chest harness also has clip-in points on the front of the chest and center of the back. This gives the students the opportunity to clip in in a variety of places and experiment with the movement and shape making opportunities they present. Unfortunately this harness meant giving up some freedom of motion. The waistband is so wide and so padded that it prevents much movement at the waist. It forces the body into a sitting position so I feel as if I am fighting the nature of the apparatus when I plank or invert in alignment. It restricts efforts to shift the pelvis to the left or right which makes running side to side, somersaults or backflips to the sides and any assortment movements of the like, difficult. The risers are connected with thick, strong bands of material that keep the leg loops in place and allow little movement between the legs and the pelvis areas. This can be tiresome during rest periods while still rigged where the only relief from groin or thigh strain comes from moving the leg loops down the legs. For relief in this harness you have to come down off the wall and put your weight in your legs. Although this presents some issues when it comes to class time and progressing through the exercises, I felt that the peace of mind acquired due to all of the safety features was worth the time cost. The harness is quite heavy and, for those experienced in aerial dance, it can feel restrictive. Over time, I began reserving these heavier more restrictive harnesses for beginners and used the more flexible harness options for more experienced dancers. More recently, when prepping to teach an aerial class I researched harnesses again (harnesses are constantly in development so checking back time and time again is a great way to stay up with current research and development in safety and comfort) and found what I feel is a wonderful compromise between safety and flexibility. I purchased a Robertson Zip Tour harness. These are commercial grade harnesses that are designed for zipline or aerial tours in adventure parks. I like them because they have a traditional sit harness with all adjustable and double backed straps and, in addition, contain an attached chest harness that has double backed adjustable arm straps as well as a chest strap. This purchase provides safety for upright and upside down activity but also allows for freedom in both the legs and the torso. The particular model I purchased does not have padding, which caused soreness among the students the first few weeks, but they adjusted over time. Some of the students felt that the clip-in belay point was a bit larger than the old climbing harnesses and therefore gave them less control. They chose to clip in to the belay point as well as the waist belt (with the same carabiner using a threading motion), which brought the carabiner closer to the body and allowed for more control. According to our rigger, threading like this through a loop and a strap is safe as long as the carabiner is auto locking and isn't cross-loaded. Check with your own rigger, though, before attempting to clip in in unusual ways.

Carabiner

The carabiner is the metal, pear-shaped, triangular, oval or D-shaped device that connects your harness to the rope via a gate containing a screw lock. Initially I used a traditional screw gate carabiner, which contains a hinged gate that snaps shut but requires the dancer to screw the gate closed. When using those devices I use my friend and colleague James Dick's safety phrase "screw down so you don't screw up", meaning that the carabiner must be situated such that screwing it to lock it involves screwing it down. If you have to screw it up to lock it, then the

Figure 1.06
Carabiner
Credit: © Washington and
Lee University 2016

carabiner is attached upside down. The phrase helps to get the carabiner situated correctly. This can be particularly helpful for left-handers, like myself who may tend to do things upside down or backwards. This is an instance where human interaction with the machinery can create safety issues. Because of this, I have gradually phased automatic locking carabiners into my equipment. By having automatic locking carabiners you cut the opportunity for mistakes. Initially all of my carabiners were aluminum, which is strong but light. I believe that new safety regulations are now being instituted by ETCP that require the use of steel carabiners in aerial theatre work. The amazing Technical Director at W&L, Tom Hackman, is now overseeing the process of transitioning my equipment to steel. You can never be too careful in aerial dance. It's important to remember that any sort of carabiner can get microscopic cracks from dropping or storing incorrectly. Be gentle. I've used Petzl and Diamondback carabiners but there are many wonderful brands out there. Just be sure to check their specs and ratings and shop at an actual outdoor store where informed climbers can answer your questions. If you see a carabiner (or any climbing equipment) at a hardware, grocery store or superstore, don't buy it. Be conservative. Assume that its sole purpose is as a key chain or adornment of some sort.

Shoes

I'm jumping out of my self imposed order here, but I must briefly mention shoes. It makes me squirm to think about my early years in aerial because I taught and performed in bare feet. I am trained as a modern dancer so it made sense to me and, I have to admit, I love to feel the wall on my feet as I move. The connection is marvelous and makes me feel truly in control of my movements. But, wow, it was a bad idea. I'm lucky that none of my students ever suffered stress fractures or broken toes. Of course it depends on the specifics of the rig, but in general, the speed and force with which an aerial dancer returns to a vertical surface after pushing off can feel like a car speeding towards a brick wall. The shock of the combined weight of your body and force of your swing creates an unhealthy impact on your bones. In my experience, the vertical spaces upon which we worked were either cinderblock or brick so the surface had no give. It was like dancing on concrete – well, it *was* dancing on concrete. That's really bad for your body in myriad ways. Even if you have the opportunity to rehearse or perform on a wooden, or sprung surface of some kind, treat the safety of your feet just as you would the safety of your head. Shoe choice is, in some ways, a personal one. I've had students who have rehearsed in super soft sneakers and loved the slipper-like feel. I don't love this type of shoe because I feel that it doesn't have enough support. Other students have liked using actual climbing shoes because they like the way the shoes grab the wall. The outer sole is usually rubber and designed to be a high friction point for climbing on rocks. They tend to be breathable. However, in my experience, the more 'feel' you get from the wall, the thinner the sole. A thin sole equates to less protection for your feet. It's important to remember that climbing shoes are designed for climbing, not for repeated impact with a hard surface. Also of note, the more aggressive the climbing shoe, the more 'pointed' the shoes are made. This is great for fitting into tiny rock cracks while climbing boulders, but if you need to flex your foot or design your foot movement at all, they can feel restrictive. Further, because the toes are aligned on top of one another in a climbing shoe, apart from feeling confining, there is a potential for spraining or breaking toes, knuckles or other tiny bones of the foot when landing with force. Apart from feeling confined, it's the recipe for disaster when landing with force. I think it's smart to find a good balance between protecting your feet and being able to move freely. I've worn trail running, hiking and tennis shoes on the wall. What an aerialist likes in terms of the feel of the wall is really personal. Just be sure that the shoes you choose are somewhat flexible but are made to withstand repeated pounding. It's the only way to ensure that your feet are adequately protected. It's difficult to require a specific shoe in an aerial class so, instead, take time to chat with your students about the best attributes of a shoe and why protection is important.

Grigri

This is a piece of equipment that, while not necessarily used in aerial performance, I have come to love and rely on completely for class. In the early days of my aerial work, we had some

Figure 1.07
Grigri
Credit: © Washington and
Lee University 2016

insane methods to get onto our vertical surface. I'm ashamed to admit that in the earliest of days, we tied into a rope on the ground, then ran the rope through a pulley system to the top of the building and then back down again. We then attached the end of the rope to the rear of a car, which we would then drive away to raise the dancers. Don't EVER do this . . . I can't believe how stupid I was! I later got marginally smarter and began rehearsal with the dancer on the roof of the building, which she rappelled down to get into place. Although safer, this was inefficient for my needs because we were rehearsing on an office building and so to repeat the phrase or dance, the dancer had to unhook from the rig, run around the building (which was the size of a small block), go in through the front door, run up six flights of stairs, go into an attic-like space, climb a ladder to the roof, walk across the roof and climb a second ladder that led to the peak of the brick face from which she would begin the rehearsal process again. This was time consuming and the ladders were a safety hazard. When I started teaching aerial in the university, I began employing the use of scaffolding (for shorter vertical spaces). We were quite careful to create safety methods by which the dancers would clip into the scaffolding as they climbed. This worked and was safe but was cumbersome and took time. The time factor was especially a problem during performances. Audiences tend to get jumpy if they have to sit in the darkness for more then a few seconds. Finally, after taking some master classes in England (Wired Aerial Theatre in Liverpool is awesome: if you ever get a chance to take classes with them – go!), I discovered the answer to my problem: the grigri. Grigri is actually the name of a specific belay device created by Petzl but the word has sort of become synonymous with this type of equipment. (Think Kleenex for tissue.) Although technically it's considered an assisted breaker, I use it as a descender. The grigri works by passing the rope over a cam, which allows it to pass through when no weight is present, in our case, as the dancer ascends. Once weight is placed on the grigri, the cam locks and prevents descent. When desired, the dancer can open a lever and control the speed of her descent. It's very important that this device is threaded correctly. (Warning: human error can easily occur here.) More on this later.

Rope

There are two basic sorts of ropes typically used for aerial: static and dynamic. Static rope is a climbing rope that has very little to no stretch and is usually used in circumstances that involve dexterity such as lowering an injured climber, for example. Dynamic rope stretches to carry some of the impact of a fall so that if a person is falling, he isn't injured by the rope that is saving him. I always use static rope in class because I want the dancer to feel they are directing their own actions. By allowing an unknown quantity like bounce or stretch to enter the picture you give up control, which is hard enough to come by in aerial dance. New aerialists especially need something that is a constant. There are so many forces they are grappling with already that it's a relief to be able to rely on something always reacting in the same way. There are many and varied types of ropes available in climbing. I use single climbing rope, meaning the rope is designed to be used alone and not in tandem with another rope. Generally I purchase 11mm rope because, though a grigri supports a range of sizes, I like to use the largest diameter that will fit into the grigri for safety and strength (plus I'm not concerned with weight of the rope as a climber would be). Be sure to always check the safety ratings when researching rope for aerial.

I have in the past worked with airline cable and I still do for larger performances. Airline cable is strong, less prone to weaknesses and wear and tear than a climbing rope and disappears from the eye nicely which gives the illusion of flying. I have stopped using it in rehearsal because, given my circumstances, it's not convenient. When teaching class and creating choreography I need the flexibility to put the dancer anywhere on the wall I desire. Because I don't have the machinery or engineering (or funds) to create apparatuses that would allow my students to climb airline cable, I was bound choreographically by the position of the cable on the wall. One year in preparation for a performance using airline cable, I tried placing three cables of varying length at each dancer's position. We rigged one airline cable high up on the wall, one at a middle point and one low. Although this gave me more options, it still wasn't ideal. (And the dancers had to be hooked into the points via scaffolding, which we've already discussed also isn't ideal.) When I create large performances and work with a professional rigging company, we use airline cables that are attached to winches to the roof of the building on which we are performing. This allows for mechanical raising and lowering of the dancers. This is wonderful, but expensive. I've found that a performance using airline cables and winches can be successfully rehearsed for with climbing ropes and using a grigri and ascender.

The majority of my rehearsals occur indoors so weather isn't a concern. However, if you plan to use climbing ropes outside you will need to ask about the water absorption rate of the rope, details on dry treated ropes and safety measures involving water or ice logged rope. Unlike airline cables, climbing ropes can easily become abraded. Wear and tear can occur due to use by a dancer and grigri and ascenders can pull and weaken the rope. Be sure to have a professional rigger check your equipment at least once a year (more if you are rehearsing extensively). I tend to buy new rope every year to be as safe as possible, even if it doesn't appear worn.

Ascender with Foot Loop

The ascender is the partner to the grigri. The ascender helps to get the aerialist up the rope and the descender (the grigri) gradually lowers them back down to the ground. In order to aid in the ascension, I attach a foot loop onto the ascender and use that device to walk up the rope. An ascender is a D shaped mechanical device, usually made of aluminum. At the top of the ascender is a locking system that fits around and clips to the rope. The cam inside the device allows upward motion only and locks when downward forces are placed upon it. At the top of the ascender is a release. Mine is a large black slider that can be operated one handed with the thumb while gripping the ascender with the palm and fingers. The slider opens and closes the device. It's used to clip the ascender onto the rope prior to climbing and for removing it from the rope when the ascension point has been reached.

Figure 1.08
Ascender with foot loop
Credit: © Washington and
Lee University 2016

All other times, the ascender is simply slid up the rope. On the lower right (or left, if you've got a lefty version) is the rubber hand grip. Below this is a hole that is typically used by climbers for attaching the ascender to their harness when it's not in use. In my class, I take the sling, a sewn loop of very strong webbing of three feet, and feed it through the hole and loop it through itself. This creates a loop of webbing knotted to the base of the ascender and hanging about three feet below it. I use this loop as a step. It's important when purchasing an ascender to try the mechanism. Different models and styles have very different sliding releases. I have a couple of ascenders whose open/closing pathway is hidden behind it and my students still have difficulty opening it weeks into the semester. Be aware that ascenders work on a variety of rope thicknesses but not all of them. I believe that my 11mm rope is on the larger end of the widths my Black Diamond ascender can handle.

Carabiner–Swivel–Carabiner

We have now covered all of the mechanisms and machinery on and around the aerialist. At this point there is a long rope leading up to a rig in the ceiling or at the top of the vertical surface, or possibly via a pulley or other system that leads back down to the floor. Either way, the final pieces of equipment happen at the top of the rig. For my purposes, the rope is tied with a loop at the top that is hooked by a carabiner then a swivel and another carabiner. I do this for a couple of reasons. If there is no swivel, then as the aerialist swings and spins, the rope winds up around itself and either throws off the aerialist or has to be painstakingly unwound. This is frustrating when a dancer is attached but downright dangerous if the dancer dismounts with the rope in this state. The metal carabiner and grigri could spin out of control and fly around and hit someone. Adding a swivel at the top also leads to a smoother, more balanced flying style. A swivel is a steel apparatus with ball bearings. It looks like two circles or two triangles with bases mounted together. The two shapes turn independently of one another but they are attached at the base. One side can be stationary while the other spins with no noticeable friction. In the early days, I attached the swivel down near the harness but quickly found that having it farther from the dancer has the benefit of preventing fingers, hair, and clothing from getting caught up or pinched. It was nice to be able to spin quickly with the swivel point down low, but found that the difference in timing with the swivel rigged high was minimal. I currently use Black Diamond circular swivels as well as CMI triangular ones. In my opinion, it seems as though the carabiners sit better in the triangular shape but they both are functional. It's important to replace these in a timely fashion based on your use. Talk to a certified rigger about when that should be.

Gacflex

My aerial rehearsals take place in a black box theatre so our aerial dancers are rigged to the ceiling's catwalk, which runs along all four walls and across the center of the space. We had an issue of concern in the past because the catwalk floor is made of rectangular, metal grating. In order to drop down the aerial ropes and have them fall close to the wall, we had to thread them through the grating. This was of concern because the rope is made of nylon and the hole through which we threaded it was made of metal. We were concerned that over time the left to right swinging could abrade the rope. We solved this problem through the prodigious use of carpet pieces that were attached between the metal and the climbing rope. While this solution was approved and carried out by the riggers and was perfectly safe, it did give me pause. My colleagues and I felt it was a bit jerry-rigged. This year we've solved our architectural problem by using Gacflex. These are similar to spansets in that they have a strong core that is surrounded by webbing and sewn together at the ends to make a sling. Instead of nylon that is wound in continuous circles in the core, Gacflex is constructed of galvanized steel aircraft cable. (Note: This is another instance where the brand name of a piece of equipment is so well known that it is used generically.) This was easily rigged as it could be tied to the catwalk and then pushed down through the metal floor grating and attached to the carabiner with no concerns about rubbing or abrasions. We are quickly approaching the riggers' area here though. Suffice it to say that if it involves the rope and how the rope is attached, it's not your area. However, knowing the language and terms and being able to intelligently ask and understand the process cannot be overrated. You will be safest if you understand the rigging yet you allow a professional to carry it out.

RIGGING THE SYSTEM

In this section I'm going to describe how each piece of equipment is used in relationship with one another and in conjunction with a professional rigger's set up. I won't describe how a rigger does his job for two reasons: 1) I am not qualified to discuss how and why a certified rigger

Figure 1.09
Double checking the equipment

Credit: © Washington and Lee University 2016

creates the basic structure for aerial dance and 2) I don't want anyone to EVER try to do it on their own. There are many videos and online discussion forums that deal with rigging and I advise everyone to stay as far away from them as possible. In aerial dance, your foremost concern should be the safety of your students/dancers. The most basic way that you can ensure safety is to work with a rigger with a certification from a respected governing body.

For continuity, I will work in the same order as I did when describing the equipment: from dancer to top of rig. I will also insert a disclaimer here for any of you *still* thinking that you don't want to pay a professional rigger/ feel you are a DIY type of person/ generally ignore the warnings of others. This information is non exhaustive. It's not intended to be comprehensive instruction. It's meant to be used in tandem with safety instructions provided with each piece of equipment and technical notices and used by fully qualified individuals with proper training and experience. So, one last time, I will implore you to hire a rigger. Lecture finished.

Safety Helmet

Make sure that your helmet is rated for mountaineering and climbing and meets certification safety standards. It's best to be sure that the helmet you choose is rated for impacts from overhead as well as from the sides. The first thing to undertake in class is to check the helmet for damage, cracks or anything that could weaken it. Do not use the helmet if you see any wear and tear. It's important to remember too that some cracks can be microscopic. If a student takes a hard hit, retire the helmet. (And get rid of it so no one accidentally uses it again.) I once had a student who dropped a helmet to someone below who was going to catch it. He missed. It hit the ground from about 20 feet up. After giving an emotional lecture about throwing around expensive equipment, I retired it. To adjust the Petzl helmet to the fit, slide the wheels on the underneath of the hat to adjust the fit from front to back and side to side. (Helmets vary by brand but have similar components.) Slide the wheels on the underneath of the hat to adjust the fit from front to back and from side to side. It should be snug and sit directly over the eyebrows. Do not tilt the helmet backwards as it will leave your forehead unprotected. Check the chinstrap both for fit and for possible fraying, damage. It should fit snugly at your throat and the front and side straps should form a "Y" around your ears. Shake your head. Your helmet should not move. Attaching a piece of tape to the helmet to identify the user has the potential to weaken it. Chemicals and solvents in tape or paint can degrade the shell. Additionally, tape can mask tiny cracks that you need to know about. Be safe and add nothing to your helmet.

 VIDEO REFERENCE 1.1. *Helmet Fitting*

Harness

Do a visual check of the harness. Note any areas that might have abrasions, tears or other weaknesses. The best way to put on the harness without getting confused about all of the straps and loops is to hold it in front of you as you would a pair of pants. The waist strap should be horizontal and the waist buckle should be at the front. The two leg loops should be hanging directly down.

The leg loops are connected to the waist belt in the back via the risers (one to each leg). The front of the leg loops each have one buckle and a connecting strap that leads up into the tie-in loop. At the front of the harness, in descending order, is the waist belt buckle, the upper tie-in loop, the belay loop (the thickest/largest loop) and the lower tie-in loop. Around the back of the waist belt, usually in a semicircle, are gear loops. The waist belt and leg loops should *always* be threaded through the buckles. If you have a harness where they are permanent, there is no worry. But if not, do not allow the students to completely remove the belts from the buckles. This creates confusion for the next person who is using it. This goes for the risers as well. I've had students remove the risers and then reattach them backwards which makes the leg loops turn inside out and in turn places the buckles directly against the skin of the dancer. It's like a puzzle trying to fix it. While holding the harness in front of you, expand the waist and leg loops as far as you can without unhooking them. Then step down through the waist and into each leg loop. Pull the harness up onto your pelvis and tighten the waist belt. The waist belt should sit above your hip bones in the front (iliac crest). You should tighten it as much as possible. I've found that the best way to tighten the waist belt completely is to ask a friend to do it while you hold onto something stable. Because of the angle of the buckle, you probably won't have the force necessary to create a snug fit by yourself. Be sure to check that the buckle is double backed. Some harnesses will have permanently double backed buckles, but in case yours doesn't you want to be sure that the buckle is not forming an "O". I tell my students that this stands for

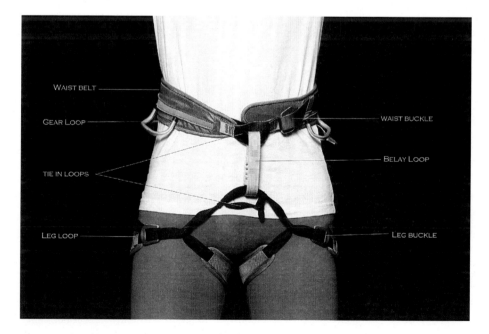

Figure 1.10 Components of a harness
Credit: © Washington and Lee University 2016

open. If you take the end of the strap and fold it backwards and put it back through the buckle, the buckle will form a "C", which stands for closed. The strap is then double backed. Be sure that the leg loops are not crossed and that the waist belt is not upside down. *Warning: human safety alert*: Having a very tight waist belt and situating it properly on your body is imperative for safety while inverting. Tighten the risers, which are now on the back of the legs, such that the leg loops fall just below the butt. Then tighten the leg loops. Leg loops should be tightened as much as possible without cutting into the legs. Check again here to be sure both leg straps are double backed. I pair my students up and have them go through a safety check on one another once the harness is on (see Safety Checklist, p. 23). Once they are tethered to the rope they also do a "sit check". This involves clipping into the rig, sitting into their harness and leaning backward. In this position, the harness will create a triangle shape with the torso. If the triangle formed between their torso and the harness is larger then their fist, they tighten the waistband. The partners also do a "pants test" where they try to pull the harness down over their partner's hips to check for proper tightness of the harness elements. If you have a chest harness it may or may not be permanently connected to the pelvis harness. Generally you simply place the straps over your shoulders and tighten each side so that you can stretch your body long but they won't fall off of your shoulders. Be sure the buckles are on the outside and the straps aren't crossed or twisted. My chest harness also has a piece that tightens across the front of the chest, just above the sternum, and helps to hold the shoulder straps in place. Note: There are harnesses specially designed for men's and women's (and children's) bodies. They vary based on center of gravity, torso rise, ratio of leg distance to pelvis, waist shape and other factors. Be sure to try them on and hang in them awhile before choosing what is best for you. I have a variety of makes and models in the dance studio.

Carabiner

Carabiners come in a variety of shapes but generally they are either triangular shaped, D shaped or oval. Though not always, they usually have a small end and a larger end. I've heard that, for climbers, the smaller end should be attached to the metal (or fabric) ring (belay loop) on the front of the harness and the larger end should be up, facing the top of the vertical surface. However, I've also heard (from my rigger) that which end is up doesn't really make a difference given our set up and type of use. What matters is that the locking mechanism is away from your body, facing out to the wall. I've found that the best way to attach the carabiner to ensure that its up-to-down and front-to-back facings are correct is to grasp it in my right hand with the smaller end of the carabiner down, open the auto locking door, turn it so that it's facing me and then slide it towards myself through the grigri opening and keep rotating it downward and hook it on the inside of the harness belay loop. This ensures that the locking mechanism is away from your body. As a left hander, I've gotten my carabiner upside down and backwards so many times that I've trained myself to attach it with my right hand. (Side note: I've found that, depending on the harness, clipping into the belay loop only can leave room for sliding and slipping between the carabiner and loop.) This isn't dangerous in any way but it affects the control the dancer has within the confines of their equipment. Sometimes I clip into all three front loops: the bottom tie in loop, belay loop and upper tie in loop. This gives me a more secure fit without any added movement. (I double checked with my rigger to ensure that this was safe for my use. If you want to try this, please do the same.) Be sure that the carabiner is not cross loaded. There are times, especially in the middle of class, when a carabiner can shift from perpendicular to the floor to parallel with the floor. If this happens immediately stop and adjust. The strength of the carabiner is compromised when it is cross-loaded. Before you ascend the wall, squeeze check the carabiner. Wrap one hand around the carabiner. Press the locking gate and the back of the carabiner together. If nothing moves, it's closed and locked.

 VIDEO REFERENCE 1.2. *Attaching Carabiner*

Grigri

Check over the grigri to be sure there are no cracks or breaks. You will attach the carabiner to the grigri but first you will need to thread it. Slide open the grigri. You will see a curved metal piece inside. To thread the rope correctly, the portion of the rope that leads to the floor should

Figure 1.11
Proper threading of a grigri
Credit: © Washington and Lee University 2016

be threaded through the end of the grigri with the picture of the hand. There is a helpful graphic drawn directly on the belay device. There is an image of a hand at one end and the image of a person climbing at the other. The rope that leads to the top of your vertical surface must be threaded through the end of the grigri with the drawing of the person. This can be confusing for those that are left-handed. I've found that the easiest solution is not to try to convert it for lefty but just to thread it right handed. Once threaded, close the grigri and attach the carabiner to your harness through the hole on the descender. It's facing the correct direction if the rope from above threads into the front of the machine. Excess rope comes out of the back of the grigri to your right and the black handle opens toward you on your left. The booklet that comes with the grigri has great pictures of how all this works. Be sure to read it carefully. Now your connection is harness, carabiner, grigri. I have my students test the grigri before ascending by raising up on tip toes and pulling the rope taut through the grigri and then sitting into their harness. If the grigri catches and holds you, you've threaded it correctly. It's important to note that the grigri is created to work when there is weight on it. If you stand on the floor and push the grigri down the rope, it will move. This is because it's not holding your weight. As you ascend, you pull the excess rope and it's fed through the grigri. More on this process later.

 VIDEO REFERENCE 1.3. *Attaching Grigri*

Rope

I've already written about types of rope and sizes. The installation of the rope will be accomplished by your rigger. Be sure to do a visual check of the rope before you ascend. Grigris and ascenders can pull and tear at the rope over time so the state of your rope should be monitored. As an added security measure, before climbing up the rope, tie a knot in the loose end. Tie it up far enough so that if you are hanging upside down and your grigri fails, you won't hit your head on the floor. This way, if for some reason your rope is too short or if your descender fails, no part of you will hit the floor. The knot will stop the rope from entering the grigri and thus add an extra layer of mechanical error protection. Once you have climbed to the required height you will put a second knot in the rope as a back up for the lower knot. You can never be too careful.

Ascender with Foot Loop

Check over the ascender for small cracks. Open and close the locking system and be sure that it moves smoothly and with minimal effort. Do a visual check of the foot loop making sure there are no tears or abrasions to the cord or in the area where the cord wraps around the ascender. Attach the ascender onto the rope. Gently pull down on the ascender to be sure it's gripping. It should not move downward at all. Be sure that the foot loop isn't knotted or tangled and is hanging vertically.

 VIDEO REFERENCE 1.4. *Attaching Ascender*

Figure 1.13 Proper ascender attachment
Credit: © Washington and Lee University 2016

Figure 1.12 Harness, carabiner, grigri, rope attachment
Credit: © Washington and Lee University 2016

GETTING ON (AND OFF) THE WALL

Once all the equipment is checked and attached properly, double check that you have a safety knot in the lower portion of your rope. To make the safety loop take a portion of the rope and double it over itself so you have two straight lines of rope side by side that are attached by the loop you created. Grab both lines and wrap them around themselves in a circle and pull through. Check the ropes to be sure they are side by side in the knot. Pull them tightly so there is no slack. You can now ascend the wall.

This process uses the ascender and the descender in tandem. If you are right handed, your right hand should be on the ascender that you have correctly attached to the rope, and your left hand should be on the rope coming out from the back of the grigri. Step one: slide the ascender up the rope a few feet. Step two: holding on to the ascender with your right hand, step up into the sling loop with your right foot. Step three: while standing in the sling loop pull the excess rope through the grigri with your left hand until it is taut. Step four: sit in your harness (the grigri will close and hold you) and take your foot out of the loop. Although it seems small, this is an important step. If you don't remove your leg from the loop, the weight of your leg will stay on the ascender and you won't be able to slide it up the rope.) Repeat, beginning at step one. Keep going until you are at your desired height.

 VIDEO REFERENCE 1.5. *Ascending the Rope*

Once at your desired height, tie the safety knot on the rope coming out from the back top of the grigri. This is an extra safety measure in case the grigri fails mechanically. The tie off is the same as the lower safety knot. As a reminder: take the loose rope coming out of the grigri and double it over itself so you have two straight lines of rope side by side that are attached by the loop you created. Grab both lines and wrap them around themselves in a circle and pull through. Check the ropes to be sure they are side by side in the knot. Pull them tightly so there is no slack.

 VIDEO REFERENCE 1.6. *Safety Knot*

Remove the ascender from the rope. If you are not too high on the wall, you can lower the ascender, metal end first, to a person on the ground. If you are quite high, pull up the rope that is coming out the back of the grigri and attach the ascender to the end of the rope and slowly lower it, metal end first. It's important not to lower the ascender sling end or rope end first because the weight of the ascender will swing and come crashing down on the person below. Be gentle with the ascenders, if they are dropped they can develop microscopic cracks that will create safety risks. Once you are rid of the ascender (you won't need it again unless you plan to climb higher at a later time) coil up the length of loose rope that passed through the threads of the grigri. It can easily be stored by threading it through the equipment hooks on your harness. (I *knew* we'd find a use for those at some point!) When you are finished on the wall, first untie your safety knot. The grigri has a little black handle that opens and allows you to descend the rope at your own pace. In climbing this is called assisted breaking. The less open the grigri, the more the rope is pinched and the slower you will descend and vice versa. Be careful to keep your free hand (the one not working the break) clear from the grigri. As an extra security measure, thread the rope through your free hand at hip level. I've seen many students get burned by the rope when descending faster then expected so thread it through *very* loosely or create a bit of slack before threading for maximum protection from burns. If you are a beginner, descending the rope takes practice and a good feel for the machinery. Practice from a low height so that you aren't afraid of getting stuck up high where help can't reach you. As opposed to climbing where you have a partner who is belaying you, with a grigri you are belaying yourself. It takes coordination. Practice. Practice. Practice.

 VIDEO REFERENCE 1.7. *Descending the Rope*

SAFETY CHECKLIST

Because there is so much information concerning safety and because all of it is vitally important, the Technical Director at the university, Tom Hackman, and I created a safety checklist. I partner my students up for the duration of the semester and make them responsible for their own safety as well as the safety of their partner. Each student is responsible for getting into their own harness and checking their materials and equipment. In addition to this, in every class I hand out a safety checklist and each person fills it out for their partner. In this way every student is checked twice: once by themselves and once by another person. (Before they go onto the wall, I give them their third check.) By filling out the form and checking each safety element, the students not only double check one another's work but also learn, over time, all of the steps necessary for a safe flight. At some point in the semester, the students invariably begin to "forget" to fill out the safety checklist. They become familiar with the class and the equipment and their fear slowly ebbs away. This is sometimes a difficult period. The students are having fun. They love aerial and want to be part of the class because of the exciting elements and their desire to push the limits of the form. However, this is the exact right time to stop everything and spend time reiterating the importance of safety procedures. I go into more detail about how each element contributes to the overall safety of the aerialist and I double down on the filling out of the safety checklist. Depending on the arrogance of the students involved, I am, sometimes, forced to lecture on real world aerial accidents and the physical ramifications of accidents involving aerial dance. I don't do this to scare them (except a little bit, I do). Honestly, depending on the type of student in the class, they may need to be scared. No one is allowed on the wall if I feel they are being unsafe or not respectful of the rig. This is reflected in their grades as well. Sometimes that alone is enough to scare them.

The aerial safety checklist can be downloaded from the aerial dance companion website. To keep things organized and to have a record of what we've done, each set of partners has a clipboard. After they fill out their forms for one another and I approve their form, they clip it to the board and it gets stored in the wooden aerial storage box drawer.

 REFERENCE ONLINE INFORMATION 1.0 *Aerial safety checklist*

SAFETY TEST

In addition to the safety checklist, I require every student who wishes to dance vertically to take a written safety test. This test is given after all of their safety lectures are complete and after they've had a chance to put on a harness and learn the set up and how to work the equipment. Every student is required to get 100% on the test before they are allowed on the wall. They may take the test more then once. Their grade is not reflected as part of the course. The purpose here is to educate them about aerial safety, not to trick them or encourage them to cram the information into their brains as fast as possible. In fact, I suggest they test one another (based on the notes they took during the lectures) prior to taking the written test so that they can really absorb the information. I try to create a situation where the safety become second nature.

The test I give can be found in Appendix A, as well as downloaded from the aerial dance companion website. It changes somewhat from year to year as regulations change and as I learn through experience from year to year what students tend to overlook and what elements need reinforcing. The answers can be found online as well.

 REFERENCE ONLINE INFORMATION 1.1 *Aerial safety test*

 REFERENCE ONLINE INFORMATION 1.2 *Aerial safety test answers*

EQUIPMENT CARE

The length of time your equipment lasts and the measure of its safety can be directly attributed to its care, handling and storage. Most of the equipment is either steel or aluminum so it's easy to be lulled into feeling that they are indestructible. These pieces are only as strong as your diligence in caring for them. Ascenders, descenders, helmets, and carabiners can all develop cracks that are undetectable to the human eye. Although it seems that nothing can hurt them, drops, hits and falls can damage them in small ways that lead to larger consequences. Additionally, all aerial pieces have a natural life that needs to be respected. The lifespan of the equipment depends upon the conditions under which it is used and stored as well as the frequency of use. When in doubt about replacing equipment, always err on the side of caution.

The life of a harness is 5–7 years with minimal use. For professional climbers, the recommendation is one year. Always check for abrasions, tears and damage. Harnesses should be stored in a protective bag away from sharp objects to prevent pulls and tears. If they get sweaty or wet, allow them to air dry before storing in a dry, dark place. The recommendation for the life of a helmet that has never seen any damage or dents is ten years. I replace mine every five years unless an accident occurred or there are signs of cracks or damage. Check inside the helmet for degradation of webbing or sizing wheels or panels and be sure the chinstrap is non-abraded and in good working order. Store helmets in a bag to keep away from sharp objects and sunlight. (Exposure to sunlight weakens the shell.) Manufacturers of aluminum and steel mechanisms (carabiners, ascender, descender) claim unlimited life for their metal products under perfect conditions. But they note that, depending on a variety of factors, any of the equipment may last one use. Check for abrasions, cracks, dents, and wear. Be sure no part is bent, scratching another part, sticky or stiff. All closures, screws and locking systems should move smoothly and easily. All elements should close completely. If necessary, clear dust or dirt out of the parts and away from the mechanisms. It is also recommended to keep them away from chemicals and extreme heat. Slings are recommended for replacement from anywhere between one year and ten years depending on use. There are a lot of places online that show photos of slings in various states and their recommended life based on the way they look. However, I feel, if there are abrasions, you should replace them.

There are many variables when it comes to the life of your equipment. To be safe, we keep a list of all the equipment and record the date purchased, model and style. We show all of the equipment to the rigger during his annual inspection and discuss the length of time we've owned it, how often it's used and any other relevant factors. I keep all of the equipment in protective bags inside a specially made wooden storage unit on wheels. It is well ventilated, out of sunlight, kept cooled/heated within appropriate limits, is kept away from harsh chemicals or abrasives and can be locked.

INSURANCE/WAIVER OF LIABILITY/ASSUMPTION OF RISK

Last but by no means least in this chapter, is all the legal stuff. You may feel that this subject is a total snooze, but pay attention. It really is of the utmost importance. If you are going to teach classes or hold a performance you need to research your insurance carrier way in advance. There are many companies that simply won't insure aerial dance. For some carriers, it's just too new a form. They aren't sure if or how it differs from circus acts and, if they do know that it carries risks, they aren't too sure of what those risks are. So they stay away. Other carriers treat aerial dance like a high wire act with no nets and are quite expensive. In the past, I've had to pay $500 to insure a three-day workshop in aerial. When I am teaching aerial for the university, I feel quite fortunate in that they handle the insurance. I know this because I've met with them, asked questions and I've worked with their insurance carrier and their lawyers to get it all ironed out. Don't assume that this will be true for you, however. Do your homework and do it well ahead of time. If you are rehearsing a show for months and months and only look into insurance for the performance venue the week prior, it may derail all of your plans. There may not be a performance. You should have insurance whether you are hosting a master class, a weekend workshop, a yearlong class or any sort of performance event. It's a good idea to look into general liability insurance. This type of insurance can cover medical expenses, lawyer fees and damages. You might want to look into property insurance or personal liability insurance as well. Most of the time accidents that occur are the result of human error – that's you. Even if the person that didn't lock the carabiner was your student, it's still your responsibility. There are so many things that could go wrong in an aerial class from rigging to equipment to student errors. You have to be diligent in outlining and following up on all of the safety measures in class and one of these is a safety measure for yourself – securing insurance.

Secondly, you absolutely must work with a lawyer to create an assumption of risk/waiver of liability form. This document states that the person partaking in the activity (if they are 18 or over) or the parent or guardian (if they are under 18) understands that aerial dance has risks that are unavoidable. This form outlines those risks. It's a little frightening, quite frankly, because it lists things like permanent injury, trauma and death. It promises that unless the person in charge is grossly negligent, they promise to release the instructor/choreographer from any liability, should the worst happen. Sometimes the waiver may also contain language that states that, should the person participating get injured, you will not pay for their medical expenses or insurance costs. It basically makes the participant (or his/her parents) aware of what they are getting into. This may cost a little bit but write it into your budget. It's worth it.

CHAPTER 2

Floor Barre
The Warm Up

As with all dance forms, warming up for aerial is very important. It goes without saying that supple, warm muscles are less prone to injury and are more prepared for work. Warming up increases blood flow to the muscles, heart, and connective tissues. It wakes up the cardiovascular system, raises body temperature and prepares the body for work. (It also helps to get rid of all the lactic acid from the previous class/rehearsal.)

Because aerial dance relies so heavily on abdominals and lower back muscles, I make sure to tailor my warm up so that the aforementioned areas have increased blood flow without working them too hard. In the early days, I included a series of intense abdominal and back strengthening exercises, thinking that these areas need to be strengthened for aerial work. However, I learned over time that, if these muscles are fatigued before going onto the wall, the length of time a dancer can stay rigged is very limited. Furthermore, if executed correctly, the very act of learning and rehearsing aerial will do the job of strengthening the core. This is not the case, however, for the biceps and triceps as the arms perform limited work in aerial dance. This is attributed to the fact that the rope and harness is holding the dancers' weight. It's important to have a strong upper body because, many times, the aerialist is catching, holding or stopping her/himself with their arms. Since they are relatively free of strain while on the wall, I do employ a rather lengthy warm up and strengthening routine for the arms and shoulder girdle. The same holds true for the hamstrings. Little attention is paid to this area while on the wall, due to the limitations of the apparatus. Unless the aerialist is high up on the wall, where tension between the dancer and the rope is strong, there is little opportunity for using this vertical surface as a means of stretching. Because the body is cold at the start of class, I save deep stretching for the end of class, following the wall exercises. At that time, the muscles are flooded with blood. They are very warm and prepared to work. (One of the best ways to injure a dancer is to intensely stretch while cold.) Some areas of the body, like the neck and shoulder region can get very tense and tight, especially in new students who haven't yet discerned the correct use of those muscles. This often leads to premature fatigue. I include stretching and lengthening periods within the warm up and cool down for these areas. In my experience, as the aerialists gain more abdominal and lower body strength, they

Figure 2.01 Abdominal and lower back areas should be warmed but not fatigued
Credit: © Washington and Lee University 2013. Also used with permission from the Corcoran Gallery of Art

stop relying on their necks to hold them up. (Using the wrong set of muscles to complete an action due to weakness in the correct set is one of those unconscious acts that dancers tend to engage in. It is comparable to looking at the floor to help them remember steps. Not only does it not help, it hurts.) I do a bit of ideokinesis at the start of class to initiate the dancers into an embodied approach to moving through space. I've found that the use of imagery aids in the transition from visual cognitive approaches in alignment to one where alignment and integration of body parts fluctuate based on various forces and pulling of the body and are understood kinesthetically.

The following is a list of warm up exercises that I've shaped over time to reflect the physical needs of the aerialist and to show what is necessary for safety and anatomically sound alignment practices. This first section of warm ups happens on the floor. I begin class here on purpose, to ensure that we are starting from a familiar place. We use the time on the floor to work in tandem with gravity and to warm up areas of the body that may not necessarily see a lot of attention once on the wall. I always have my students wear their harnesses for warm ups so that they can feel the way that their bodies interact with the device. Over time they learn the ways in which the harness restricts them and where the points of freedom lie. At times we force the harness into specific shapes to mimic the way we behave with them on the wall. The sequences can be viewed online via the video references. (For aid with terms, refer to Appendix B: Vocabulary and Appendix C: Terminology, located at the end of the book.)

Figure 2.02 Visualizing movement improves kinesthetic knowledge
Credit: © Washington and Lee University 2011

SPINE AND CORE

Begin in constructive rest. In this position you are flat on your back with your knees bent and raised up so that your feet are flat on the floor and resting directly below your knees. Line up your heels with the ischial tuberosities (sit bones). Knees are aligned and not crossing the center line. Arms are out to the sides and angled little bit lower than your shoulders so that the scapulae remain aligned. Palms are facing up. Release your body into the floor. Close your eyes. Soften your muscles and drop your bones down. Visualize your spine and its relationship to the floor. Note the natural curves anteriorly in the cervical vertebra, posteriorly in the thoracic vertebra and the larger anterior curve in the lumbar. Finally visualize the sacrum curves to the posterior. In your mind, focus on the cervical area of your spine. Be aware of any tension that you may be harboring in the cervical area. Soften. Allow the muscles to feel as if they are dripping off the bone. Let go. Shift your focus to the center of your back – the thoracic region. Be aware of any problem areas where you may feel tightness, soreness or stiffness. Think about the warmth of the floor radiating up through your skin and deep into the tissues of the spine. Allow your body to soften in the warmth. Give in to the pull of gravity. Shift your focus down to your lower back: your lumbar. Are there areas of pain? Lactic acid build up? Do you have stress or strain from sitting or poor posture? Actively release into these areas. Allow the stress to flow away from your body. Give in to the floor. Finally, feel your sacrum wide and strong against the floor. Gently shift your pelvis (contraction and release) so that the sacrum slowly rocks forward and backward. Allow this motion to encourage the length of your spine to soften and let go. Come back to a place of rest. Be aware of your spine in it's entirety. Feel it long from the base of your skull all the way down to your coccyx (tailbone). Be aware of the points of connection between the floor and your body. Where do they touch? Where do they separate? Slide your focus to your lumbar. If it is not in contact with the floor, shift your pelvis and engage your abdominals and lower back so that your lumbar is flat. In most cases this will involve pushing against your harness to achieve the desired shape. Release. Come back to constructive rest. Note the difference between your lumbar at rest and your lumbar in alignment. Repeat as necessary. Press your lower back into the floor, press your belly button to your spine, and engage your abdominals and lower back muscles. Be aware of the connection between your body and the floor. You may need to push against the harness in this position as it's designed to make you sit upright. Keep hollowing out in your abdominals as you slowly lift your tailbone off the floor. Curl in your lumbar as you roll up your back. Your pelvis is lifting up. Press all the way up, pushing through the harness. Over time you will begin to develop muscle memory for this position. When you are planking against the wall, these are the muscles you will use for an aligned torso. Slowly lower down one vertebra at a time. Keep lifting the tailbone up as you release down. Feel the muscles around each vertebra warming. Release and soften all the way down through your spine. When you reach the bottom of your lumbar, down through your coccyx, you can relax. Let your body come back to constructive rest. Repeat as needed.

 VIDEO REFERENCE 2.1. *Spine and Core*

LEGS AND FEET

From the constructive rest position, pull your right knee into your chest. Feel your harness pushing against the legs. Reach around and grasp below the knee on both sides. Push the knee away from the hip with your quadriceps as the hands/arms hold and push in. Allow the acetabulum to open and breathe. Hold. Soften in and around the acetabulum (inside the hip where the head of the femur meets the pelvis) and along the quadriceps, press the knee into the chest for a stretch. Repeat as needed. Extend the leg to the ceiling. Flex your foot if you can. Be gentle as you aren't warm yet. Feel your hamstrings begin to work. This position is employed on the wall many times when we sit in the harness and face the wall with legs outstretched. Gravity will be working in a different way on the wall. However, over time a muscle memory will form that will aid in achieving this position correctly with the appropriate musculature. Press your foot through forced arch, point the foot, pull toes back into forced arch again, flex foot. Repeat as necessary with varying speeds. Release behind the knee and allow the knee to fall into your chest. Reach around the knee with both arms, grab and push for the stretch. Repeat the entire exercise on the other leg. Come back to constructive rest. Be sure the arms are out to the sides, angled slightly below the shoulders with palms up. Soften into the floor. Release down. Reengage the abdominals and lower back, pressing the belly button down into the spine. Torso is zipped from pubic bone to sternum. Core is strong. Drop both knees to the right. As the weight of the legs shifts, don't allow the torso to disengage. Keep upper and lower abdominals engaged and shoulders flat on the floor. The top leg slides along the floor, staying on the floor with a bent knee swinging the leg up to the shoulder. The leg then slides back down, the floor completely taking the weight of the leg as it scoops back down, joins the other leg and both knees swing up and arrive back where they started (in constructive rest). Repeat on other side. Repeat at varying speeds on both sides as necessary. (Note: it's important that the weight of the legs is supported by the floor. This warm up is specifically designed to work the muscles in and around the psoas. If the dancer takes the weight of the leg, the quadriceps engage and the psoas does not get warm.) Come back to constructive rest. Release down into the floor.

 VIDEO REFERENCE 2.2. *Legs and Feet*

Drop your right knee out to the side and cross your ankles such that the right ankle is on top of the left foot. The leg that's bent swings out to the side, maintaining contact with the floor until the very end, where it lifts off the ground at ear height for a hamstring stretch. The leg then slowly lowers and returns to its crossed position over the ankle. In this exercise it's important that the pelvis and shoulder girdle stay flat on the ground. Do not allow the movement of the leg to affect the alignment of the pelvis. The neck/chin is released so that the face is pointing directly at the ceiling. Release the shoulders. Repeat on right side eight times and then switch to the left side. This can be done slow for control, and later, a bit faster, using momentum for more of a swing. (But be careful here as the hamstrings really aren't warm yet.) Come back to constructive rest. Extend the body flat into an "X" position, reaching the arms out near the ears on a 45 degree angle from the head and legs straight down on a 45 degree angle from the central axis line. Relax the legs. Engage arms, reaching them far away from the torso, creating space within the shoulder sockets, engaging the muscles of the arms by reaching away from the center axis. The abdominals are engaged from pubic bone to sternum. Press your lumbar down into the floor. The torso is strong. Relax. Repeat with the legs, reaching out of the acetabulum, creating space by elongating within the hip girdle. Relax. Repeat the exercise with the right arm pairing with the left leg. Stretch across the torso at a diagonal making sure not to arch the back. Keep pressing the abdominals and lower back down into the floor as you reach away at an angle. Repeat on the opposite diagonal.

 VIDEO REFERENCE 2.3. *Legs and Feet part 2*

HEAD AND NECK

Soften back into the "X" position and relax into the floor. Imagine the top of your head being pulled away from your body. Elongate the neck and reach the ears away from the shoulders. Create space inside your neck. Lengthen. Gently soften and release your head into the floor. Repeat. Engaging behind and in front of the neck, raise the head off the floor and curl your chin into your chest. Gently release your head back down releasing one vertebra at a time and working sequentially. Repeat. Repeat but at top flexion, use the weight of hands on top of the head to press forward and extend the stretch a little. Repeat. Soften into the "X" position again. Gently slide your head from the central axis to the right arm, keeping the head in contact with the floor and the face up to the ceiling. If needed, use the right arm to extend the stretch a little by placing your hand around the head and grasping the opposite ear to provide a small pull to the side. Be gentle. Slowly slide your head back to center. Repeat on the other side.

 VIDEO REFERENCE 2.4. *Head and Neck*

TORSO, ARMS, AND BACK

Come back to your "X" position. Moving from your core, engage the abdominals and contract the torso to the right. Left arm slides along the floor over your head and left leg slides down and around the other leg so that you roll onto the right side of the body. Pull into a fetal position on your right side. Move through the X position as you roll to the left, right arm reaches over your head and right leg reaches below the other leg as you roll onto your side. Keep rolling onto your knees, head and torso are in a ball. Push against the arms and legs so they straighten. Press your body into a triangle with the floor with your hips raised to the ceiling. Keeping your legs straight, press your sternum down into the floor. Shift your pelvis, tuck your left arm and leg and lower yourself down onto your left side in a fetal position. Open your body into an X. Arms and legs contract in and pull into a fetal position on the right side. Lengthen your torso and extend the arms and legs out, rolling onto your back and into the X position. Repeat to the other side. This can be done with ever increasing speed so that its primary purpose shifts from release and contraction to engaged, aerobic muscular contractions. Repeat as necessary, ending the final exercise in the fetal position. Unfold legs and arms so you roll onto your stomach.

 VIDEO REFERENCE 2.5. *Torso, Arms and Back*

With the front of your body in contact with the floor, tuck your toes under and place the flats of your hands next to your shoulders. Engaging your abdominals, press your belly button into your spine to engage the psoas and push up just an inch off the floor, making sure that your entire body is off the floor in a straight and aligned form. Hold. Release down to the floor and rest. Position hands out from the body a little bit. Straighten your arms into a push up position, head in alignment with the body, making sure that you are shaped like a sliding board, head highest and feet lowest. Hold. Release your elbows to the back slightly (plié with your arms) to engage your triceps. Hold. Repeat straightening and bending elbows with holds. From the push up position, push your pelvis up to the ceiling, creating a triangle shape between your body and the floor (downward dog). Release your hamstrings, release in the ankles. Push backwards within the shoulder girdle as you push the sternum down to the floor while arching in the thoracic vertebra. Pelvis goes up to the ceiling. Hold the stretch. In that triangle position, gently lower the head to the floor by releasing the elbows. Be sure that the head touches the floor between the hands in this pushup. Repeat as necessary. Walk hands backwards towards feet. Hang. Drop your head. Keep back long. Walk hands out a few steps. Lift leg off the floor in parallel so that it is in alignment with your pelvis. Point the toe. Hold. Swing leg to the side as you turn it out, forming an "L" with your supporting leg. Flex the extended foot. Be sure that the leg is parallel to the ground and your hips are squared. Two straight legs. Hold. Swing the leg in attitude up and over your pelvis. Let the leg fall behind your torso. Allow your pelvis to open to the side. Feel your abdominals stretch. Keep your shoulders squared and your head between your arms. Hold. Tuck the leg down behind the supporting leg and walk the arms back out to the push up position. Be sure your hands are directly below your shoulders and your head is in line. Your pelvis should be in line with your body, creating the shape of a sliding board. Hold. Very slowly release your arms and allow your body to slowly lower to the floor. Be careful that your body lowers as one piece, not pelvis first. Repeat all of this on the other side.

 VIDEO REFERENCE 2.6. *Torso, Arms and Back part 2*

Wall Barre

Coordination and Balance

Although this book is meant as an introduction to aerial dance, I've included both intermediate and advanced options for each set of exercises listed. In addition to these variations, it's worth mentioning that altering a combination's tempo dramatically alters its nature. When timing is sped up or slowed it affects the strength needed to create the shape and move through

Figure 3.01 Specific exercises are designed for the targeting and coordination of muscles
Credit: © Washington and Lee University 2009

space, it alters the timing of the landing and subsequent leaving of the wall and the force at which the movement occurs in space and against the wall is dramatically different. Just a simple change in timing changes an introductory lesson to one requiring advanced skill. Similarly, changing speed within a phrase, like assigning some movements in 8 counts and others in 4, requires the dancer to play with time, space and effort in new and exciting ways. When I have total beginners I tend to not work with counts at all for the first few weeks. I speak the vocabulary as they do it to keep them together. This is because, even when dealing with simple phrases, the amount of force an individual needs to exert for specific timing is dependent on their height, mass and distance up or down the wall, among other things. This then contributes to how they, for example, navigate, push away, spin through space or land. As the students progress, they begin to learn how much force their body needs to accomplish various movements at various heights and, at that point, I introduce counts.

At this point, I split the class into two groups and I harness the first group of students onto the wall. Throughout the class I alternate groups working on the wall, so each receives rest periods. I've found that frequent, short rest periods are a good way to keep the students from burning out before a 90-minute class ends.

From this point on, the exercises are designed for the targeting and coordination of muscles specific to aerial dance and exercises that aid in the development of the aerial dancer. Anatomically we deal with strength building, extension, coordination, and flexibility. Spatially, we focus on proprioception, timing, force, and energy. Using the wall for warming up is beneficial in a number of ways. It gives the student a good amount of time to get a *feel* for the wall. By feel, I mean the idiosyncratic relationship between each dancer and the vertical surface. Because each dancer will have a different height and weight with varying ratios of, for example, torso to leg length or distance from shoulder girdle to pelvis, the spatial movement relationship for each dancer will vary. The dancer will begin to experience a very specific internal understanding, and later, dialogue, so that they learn to move, balance and thrust with personal specific, distinctive parameters. Their proprioceptors will become honed and specialized to their own experience. The more time spent experiencing this phenomenon, the quicker the dancers will synthesize the rapid fire, minute or substantial changes that need to occur within themselves to respond to their changing environment.

We begin with small movements very high up on the wall. The short distance between the dancer and the top of the rig means the dancer is clipped into with a very short rope. This enables the dancer to feel "glued" to the wall. In this position, the dancer has facility to regulate his/her movements and can accomplish precise and usually smaller motions with control. Warm up exercises in this very high position feel comfortable to the experienced dancer because traditional dance warm ups are reflected in the steps and sequence of phrases. This familiarity helps the circumspect mover that might be fearful of this new experience. Warming up on the wall also puts the dancer into the aerial experience immediately. They are thrust into an environment with gravitational forces that are at odds with usual posture and movement and are being required immediately to redefine their spatial relationship to it.

Figure 3.02 Gravitational forces influence speed and motion
Credit: © Washington and Lee University 2009

I split the wall into three sectors by defining abstract lines on the wall. (There have been times when I've actually marked out the regions with tape. This can be very helpful for first time aerialists.) The highest point is as close to the top of the rig as possible while still allowing the dancer enough rope length to sit in a plank position with legs outstretched on the wall. The second position is at the middle of the wall, this allows for some pushing away from the wall due to the rope being longer but the dancer still feels somewhat in control. The third position is almost to the bottom of the wall but high enough up so that the dancer couldn't stand if she/he put their feet down. This position allows for maximum push away and airtime and is where a lot of the spinning and flipping occurs. Control is very difficult at this low level and requires an advanced understanding and application of spatial dynamics. Depending on the height of the wall and how large you want the sectors, more zones could be added. I divide the wall in this way because I structure the class such that specific exercises occur in distinct areas. For example, demi pliés are taught very high on the wall, where the dancer has compete control due to the shortness of the rope and therefore can focus on precision, alignment and balance. Large jumps that include a backward flipping motion are taught very low on the wall where the dancer has ample rope with which to push away and is challenged to control movement within her body and through the appropriate use of force. Within each region, however, there is room to tailor height to the needs of the dancers. For example, if a student has short legs and we are working in the second region, she may choose to be in the lower portion of the second section to enable her to achieve the same distance from the wall when pushing off as someone who has longer or stronger legs. In the beginning of the semester, the sectors give the students a touchstone from which to determine where they can perform a given movement successfully. Throughout the class the student develops an understanding of the variables present and how to control them. This process is quite different from one student to the next. It's a combination of the specifics of their anatomy, the idiosyncrasies of their movement style, the force they employ, how they use space and the energy they expend. Over time the students master these elements and the sectors are no longer needed. They begin to adjust naturally and compensate for any sort of placement or change in height.

In some ways, the wall exercises follow a traditional ballet warm up at the barre. Modifying established technique as a warm up serves two purposes. It is efficient and productive, meaning that its benefits have been established and are transferable to the new vertical surface. It also provides a bit of solace to dancers new to aerial. For experienced dancers, there is something comforting about the ritual of a ballet or modern warm up. In an aerial class, where the students typically feel lost at first, it is something familiar. I've found that students who've never had any dance training typically do not feel intimidated, as these modified exercises are very simple. As I watch them move, it's quite clear if I need to break down a ballet-centric word and it's simple to define it as we move through the exercise.

Unless indicated, each exercise is repeated four times. Of course this can be altered based on the experience and fitness level of your students and based on the number of exercises you choose to incorporate within the hour and a half class. It's important to not fatigue the students too early as aerial is quite demanding. Additionally, some lessons build upon themselves so multiple repetitions of each exercise may not be necessary. For questions about terminology, please refer to Appendix C: Terminology.

PREPARATION

Climb to the highest point on the wall. Sit in an L position. In this position, the body faces the wall with legs extended so that the feet are in alignment with the pelvis. Feet are in parallel. Legs are straight. Back is long and sitting tall out of the ischial tuberosities. Head reaches up towards the ceiling. Eyes look directly in front. Arms are at sides, straightened and reaching down to the floor. Energy radiates out of the fingers. Abdominals are engaged, lifted and pressed back into the spine.

Figure 3.03 L position
Credit: © Washington and Lee University 2016

EXERCISES

L to Plank

From the L position, feet in parallel, slowly lower the torso back into the plank position. Press your belly button into your spine to deeply engage your abdominals and psoas. Lengthen your lower back. Shoulders are in alignment with the torso but relaxed. Head is aligned but try not to crunch the neck muscles. Reach your head long, away from the body. Be sure that your eyes are looking directly up at the ceiling. Hold. Slowly rise up, back to the L position. Repeat.

 VIDEO REFERENCE 3.1. *Plank*

Plank with side Contraction

Release back into the plank, add a slow contraction to the right. In the contraction, keep the front of the torso and face flat to the ceiling and feet steady in place. Be careful that the pelvis doesn't shift in the opposite direction. Be aware of your alignment. Slowly release and come back to the plank position and raise up to L. Repeat with the contraction to the left.

 VIDEO REFERENCE 3.2. *Plank with Side Contraction*

Walk Down

From the L position, place feet in first position parallel. Walk down the wall in small steps and allow your body to come in towards the wall. Keep walking down until your feet are hanging and face/torso is very close to the vertical surface. Use your hands on the wall in front of you for balance. Hang. Begin to walk back up the wall in small steps until you are back in the L position. Repeat.

 VIDEO REFERENCE 3.3. *Walk Down*

Walk Down with Plank

From the L position, lower down to plank position. Walk down the wall in small steps and allow the body to come towards the wall being careful to keep the body in full alignment. The torso rises in alignment towards the wall until the feet are hanging and face/torso is very close to the wall. Hang. Begin to walk back up the wall, keeping the body properly aligned, until you are back in plank position. Repeat. After final plank, return to L position.

 VIDEO REFERENCE 3.4. *Walk Down with Plank*

Ankle Circles

Sitting in an L position, feet are in parallel. Bend the right leg at the knee and allow foot to fall below the body. Ankle circle 2× right and 2× to the left. Placing the foot back into parallel, repeat on the other foot. Bring right leg back to parallel first position. Keeping the right leg straight and in parallel, open it out to the side and form a small V with your legs. Torso stays facing the wall. Ankle circle 2× to right and 2× to left. Bring leg back to wall and repeat on the left leg. Turn out both feet into first position. Repeat entire exercise with turn out.

 VIDEO REFERENCE 3.5. *Ankle Circles*

Foot Roll and Press

From the L position, place feet in first position parallel. Roll up through R foot into forced arch, roll over the top of the foot and press over the toes stretching the top of the foot. Roll down. Repeat RLRL. Turn the feet out into first position. Repeat. Step out into parallel second position. Repeat. Change to turned out second position. Repeat.

 VIDEO REFERENCE 3.6. *Foot Roll & Press*

Press Foot with Plié

From L position, place feet in first position parallel. Roll up through the R foot to forced arch and roll down, alternating as other foot rolls up, RLRL. Demi plié and open feet to first position turned out. Repeat. Open to second position parallel. Repeat. Demi plié and open feet to second position turned out. Repeat. Change to parallel first position. Repeat entire exercise.

Intermediate: add second position arms.

Advanced: Repeat entire exercise in plank position.

 VIDEO REFERENCE 3.7. *Press Foot with Plié*

Press Foot with Plié and Relevé

From L position, place feet in first position parallel. Roll up through the R foot to forced arch and roll down, alternating as other foot rolls up, RLR. Drop heel, relevé both legs straight 2× and release down (no plié). Plié, change feet to turned out first position. Repeat in first position turned out, second position parallel and turned out, and fifth position parallel and turned out. Repeat 2×, changing to the other foot front in fifth position on the repeat.

Intermediate: Add second and fifth position arms.

Advanced: Repeat entire exercise in plank position.

 VIDEO REFERENCE 3.8. *Press Foot with Plié & Relevé*

Plié Forced Arch

From L position, place feet in first position parallel. Flex knees into demi plié, relevé both feet into forced arch position, straighten legs into relevé in forced arch, plié both legs still in forced arch, drop the heels, straighten legs. Repeat 2×. Repeat in turned out first position. Repeat in parallel and turned out second position and fifth position.

Intermediate: Add second and fifth position arms.

Advanced: Repeat entire exercise in plank position.

 VIDEO REFERENCE 3.9. *Plié Forced Arch*

Tendu

From L position, place feet in first position parallel. Tendu front (up the wall) in parallel, rotate leg to turn out and rotate leg back in, return leg to first position. Repeat. Repeat two times to the side and to the back. (On tendu to the back, reach foot down the wall demi plié on the front leg.) Repeat entire exercise on the left side.

Intermediate: Add second and fifth position arms.

Advanced: Repeat entire exercise in plank position.

 VIDEO REFERENCE 3.10. *Tendu*

Jogs with Hop

From L position, with feet in first position parallel, jog 3× (RLR) hop R. Repeat two times alternating feet. Turn out feet and repeat. Repeat entire exercise in second position. Repeat entire exercise in fifth position R&L.

Intermediate: Add second and fifth position arms.

Advanced: Repeat entire exercise in plank position.

 VIDEO REFERENCE 3.11. *Jogs with Hop*

Jogs with Echappé:

From L position, feet in first position parallel, jogs 4× échappé out to second position plié and in. Repeat 2×. Repeat in turned out first position 2×. Repeat entire exercise from fifth position R&L parallel and turned out. (In fifth position, échappé into wider fifth position, not second.)

Intermediate: Add second and fifth position arms.

Advanced: Repeat entire exercise in plank position.

 VIDEO REFERENCE 3.12. *Jogs with Echappé*

Jogs with Plié and Relevé

From L position, with feet in first position parallel, jog 3×, (RLR), relevé R, drop heel R, put other foot down, demi plié. Repeat 2×. On final demi plié, change to turned out first position and repeat 2×. Repeat exercise in second position. Repeat exercise in fifth position. Repeat entire exercise on the left.

Intermediate: Add second and fifth position arms.

Advanced: Repeat entire exercise in plank position. Plank position with arms.

 VIDEO REFERENCE 3.13. *Jogs with Plié and Relevé*

Rond de jambe

Lower the torso into a plank position, parallel with the floor. Be sure to press your pelvis into your harness to achieve a flat back. Engage your abdominals pressing back into your spine and lengthen through the top of your head. Feet in parallel. Keeping your body parallel with the ceiling, extend your R leg forward toward the wall and up to the ceiling so that it is perpendicular with your torso, slowly carry it to the side making sure that your torso, and specifically pelvis, doesn't shift. Close into first. Bring your leg directly out to the side, raising it off the wall making sure to stay in alignment, draw the leg to the back (down the wall) as you gently plié on the 'standing' leg. Touch the wall with the toe and draw the leg back in to first position. Repeat on the other leg. Repeat entire exercise turned out.

Intermediate: Entire exercise with arms in second position.

Advanced: Entire exercise with arms in fifth position.

 VIDEO REFERENCE 3.14. *Rond de jambe*

Battements

From L position, place feet in first position parallel. Using both hands, grab onto the rope above the carabiner. DO NOT grab the grigri or the carabiner. Bend the right leg at the knee, dropping the foot below the body. Swing torso forward towards the rope. Bring leg forward, skimming the wall and, as the leg rises into the air release the torso backward into plank to allow full upward movement in the leg. Release the leg back down and bring torso up to the rope. Repeat 4×. Side: bend R leg so that knee points out to the R side and leg tucks behind supporting leg. Swing leg out to the side and allow torso to open to the R, keeping the alignment of the torso and pelvis intact. Bring leg back in, skimming the wall. Bend the knee to repeat 4×. Back: bend R leg so that knee comes into the chest, while extending torso to the back to plank. Swing leg down, skimming the wall and reaching behind as the torso comes forward towards the rope. Bring leg back pulling into the chest to repeat 4×. Repeat entire exercise on the left.

Intermediate: Repeat the entire exercise in turned out positions.

Advanced: Do not hold on to the rope.

 VIDEO REFERENCE 3.15. *Battement*

Pliés: Demi and Grande

From L position, place feet in parallel, arms down to the sides. Demi plié 2×, grande plié 1×. Repeat. Shift feet to turned out first position and repeat. Shift feet to parallel second position and repeat. Shift feet to turned out second position and repeat. Shift feet to parallel fifth position and repeat. Repeat in fifth position turned out. Repeat entire exercise on the left side.

Intermediate: Add arms out to sides on second position and arms up next to ears for fifth position.

Advanced: Do entire exercise in plank position with arms.

 VIDEO REFERENCE 3.16. *Plié*

Jumps

First Position

From L position, place feet in parallel, hands holding the rope above the grigri. Demi plié, and small jump that comes a few inches off the wall. Repeat 4×. On last jump, bring heels together in the air and land turned out in first position. Repeat small jumps in turned out first position 4×. Staying in first position turned out, big push off the wall and allow legs to kick out diagonally to the front in a V position, bringing legs back into first position upon landing. Repeat 2×.

Second position

On last large jump of first position, bring feet into parallel in the air and land in parallel second position. Small jumps 4×. On last jump, turn out heels in the air and land in turned out second position. Small jumps 4×. Larger jump pushing off the wall and allow legs to kick out to the sides in a wide straddle position. Repeat 2×.

Fifth position

On last large jump of second position, bring feet into parallel in the air and land to repeat in fifth position, right foot front. Small jumps 4×, alternating sides with changement. At last jump, turn out heels in the air and land in turned out fifth position. Small jumps 4×, alternating sides with changement. Make a larger jump pushing off the wall and allow right leg to kick forward and left leg to kick back in a fifth position split. Repeat 2×. On last jump, repeat entire exercise in fifth position left leg front. On last big jump of fifth position, bring feet into parallel in the air and land in first position.

Intermediate: Do entire exercise in plank position.

Advanced: Do entire exercise in plank position and do not hold on to the rope.

 VIDEO REFERENCE 3.17. *Jumps*

Stretches

Quad Stretch

In L position, grab rope with L hand and bend the L knee and grab foot with right hand, reaching behind your back to grab the toes. Pull foot backward, stretching the quad and, at the same time, lean backward straightening the arm that is holding the rope. Keep the head in alignment looking up to the ceiling. Hold. Repeat on the other side.

 VIDEO REFERENCE 3.18. *Quad Stretch*

Split

In L position, make a small jump and split legs into either two straight legs or the front leg straight and back leg bent (depending on flexibility of the student). Drop head and torso back into plank position. Hold. As the body lowers to the wall, arms reach back over head in a V. Push legs together to come back to plank and release to the other side. Repeat 8×. Return to plank and then to L position.

 VIDEO REFERENCE 3.19. *Split*

Hamstring Stretch

From L position, walk your legs up the wall to invert. Allow body to touch the wall and wrap legs around the rope. Arms out to the sides and down, touching the wall for stability. Bend knee and draw R leg down along center rope to your chest. Grab foot or calf and open leg to the side for the stretch. Keep leg against the wall. Keep pelvis flat to the wall and shoulders square. Hold. Bend the knee and place it back along the rope. Repeat with the other leg. Unwrap legs from rope. Walk back down the wall to plank. Come up to L position. Repeat.

 VIDEO REFERENCE 3.20. *Hamstring Stretch*

Back Release

From L position, walk your legs up the wall to invert. Bend knees and allow full body to touch the wall. Open legs out to a V. Let arms hang down. Hold. Bend knees and walk down the wall into a plank. Rise up to L position. Repeat.

 VIDEO REFERENCE 3.21. *Back Release*

Calf Stretch

From L position, walk your legs just a couple of steps down the wall so that, with knees bent, the ball of one foot is in contact with the wall but the heel is not. (The other foot is not on the wall. It's hanging from the harness and bent.) Straighten the leg, pressing toes against the wall and allowing hamstring and achilles to release and stretch. Hold. Plié that leg and then repeat the stretch. Repeat 4×. Switch legs and repeat entire exercise to the other side.

 VIDEO REFERENCE 3.22. *Calf Stretch*

A REMINDER

Continually remind your students throughout this warm up section, as well as the rest of the class, to keep breathing. It sounds silly but I've noticed that students get so focused on alignment, balance, and the combination itself that they quite frequently hold their breath until the exercise is over. Breathing is your best friend in aerial dance. (Well, it's always your best friend.) However, many times when the abdominals are engaged we stop breathing without realizing we are doing so. The key to strong abdominals is to be able to breathe through the contraction. The muscles need to be engaged, work and still be pliable. As a way to teach this, sometimes in the floor barre I have students lie down, engage their abdominals and lower back muscles and push their spine into the floor. (This is helpful to new dancers because they can actually feel their backs on the floor so they know if they are doing it correctly.) Then I ask them to keep their backs on the floor but release their abdominals. Some internal dickering goes on. Once accomplished, I ask them to continue to feel their spines on the floor while engaging their abdominals but releasing their back muscles. Again, some inner conversation happens. This is a great way to introduce the idea of the multi-functioning of muscles and the fact that the students can control which muscles they are using to perform a specific task. When the students feel confident with this exercise, I introduce breathing. We do the same exercise but with specific breathing patterns. This generally upsets the apple cart and the students have to re-orientate to include the new variable. It's fascinating to watch and teaches valuable lessons about the multifaceted nature and connectivity of movement and breath.

C H A P T E R   4

Center Floor

Turns and Inverting

Once the body is thoroughly warmed, we begin to move to more complex elements. This involves the blending of movement, shapes, and patterns as well as the challenge of controlling stillness and motion. These exercises tend to begin on center, move off center, use momentum, and return to stasis. For the first time, the dancer is challenged to discover a greater relationship between their body and space. There is multitasking involved that tests the spatial relationship of the dancer while also moving through a pattern of motion that requires specific placement, timing and force. Through experimentation we learn how much force is required to push the

Figure 4.01 Height, force, timing, and torque are inversion variables
Credit: © Washington and Lee University 2009

body away from the wall with a specific movement intent. Those parameters are defined through a given set of variables but with a specific desired outcome. For example, if the exercise goal is to begin in L position and push off the wall such that the shape rotates 180 degrees so the dancer's back is against the wall with legs outstretched then pushing a second time to continue the arc and return to the wall with legs straight and the body in an L shape, there are a number of factors to be considered. The height of the dancer on the wall determines the amount of rope that they are working with. The length of rope is one of the variables that determines how much force is necessary to move the body in a half turn. Also determining the half turn is the weight of the dancer, the power of the dancer, the length of the dancer's legs, and the speed at which they are required to finish, among other things. In this specific example, the first turn and second turn could be wildly different in terms of force and energy required. This is due to the fact that the motion of the first turn happens almost naturally as the feet leave the wall. The aerialist is moving from an extended position (relative to the rigging point) which, in this case, is legs straight on the wall in an L position to a flat one (again relative to the rigging point) with her back against the wall. The second turn requires not only rotation, but also a pushing away from the wall so that the legs can return without bending. This is because the movement is going from a flat position in line with the rope rig, to one that angles the rope about 45 degrees away from the wall. Spatially, the aerialist must contend with pushing with one hand away from the wall and the other hand in an angular motion to achieve both spin and outward force. Over time, the dancer learns both spatially and dynamically how to accomplish this task.

Another variable (like the aerialist needs one!) is timing. All of the exercises listed in this book can be accomplished by first applying them to some sort of consistent tempo and then performing the same exercise again, for example, in half time or double time. I mention it here because, generally, the exercises high up on the wall can be varied musically without creating too much of a challenge for the dancer. This is due to the 'sticky' relationship between the dancer and the wall that I wrote about earlier. The short rope leads to a stability that enables the dancer to move at faster or slower tempos without many complications for the dancer. When the dancer is a bit lower, however, just staying erect is a challenge. It's important to remember that timing that is too slow can be just as difficult as timing that is too fast. Speedy tempos may throw off a new aerialist's balance and transitions and cause an unintended domino effect in terms of phrasing. However, while slow tempos may seem to give the dancer time to complete movements, they generally tax the muscles which can detract from the success of the movement and potentially harm the dancer. For beginning aerialists, the teacher must try to find the perfect balance between enough speed to accomplish the task but not so much time that the muscles are straining with effort just to stay in alignment. As the dancer progresses and gets stronger, variations in tempo give the teacher options with which to challenge them. When I have new dancers that I want to challenge with music, I tend to simplify the exercise and then intensify the musical challenge. Varying these two elements gives the teacher a chance to expose new dancers to tempo without making it so difficult that no lessons are learned.

I think of this portion of the class, in general terms, as the equivalent of a traditional modern class' center and floor work segment. By this, I mean we've completed the warm up – the

Figure 4.02 Lessons in space and dynamics
Credit: © Washington and Lee University 2009

waking up of our muscles and blood flow (floor barre), done our barre work (in the case of this aerial class, the wall warm up) – meaning those exercises created with the intention of building specific muscles, and sequences of movement. We've spent time developing and honing specific skills so that movement may be accomplished with strength and grace as part of larger phrases. At this point, in traditional dance terms, the dancer is ready to move into the center of the dance floor to begin a freer set of movements that use and expound upon the skills learned previously by inviting greater space and a less controlled environment. To achieve this in aerial, we descend down the rope a little to the center area of the vertical surface. The extra length of rope gives more freedom while taking away some of the control. This requires more advanced technique and a more mature understanding of the body and how it relates to space. Below are some of the exercises I use in this portion of the class. They are ordered such that they build upon prior knowledge as the exercises progress. Note: I don't use every exercise in every class (that would be exhausting), I choose exercises that are necessary to accomplish the goals for that specific week.

Knee Turns

Beginning in L position, walk down the wall until your knees are touching it. Be sure that your hips are aligned with your knees, your knees are pressing together and your ankles are pressing together as well. Back is straight, abdominals pressing into your spine and ischial tuberosities are reaching down into the floor. Shoulder girdle is sitting directly above pelvis. Arms are long and reaching down into the floor. Push away with the top of your L toe to rotate your body in a half turn backwards over your R shoulder so that you end with your back against the wall. Be sure to maintain the sitting position. Using your R hand against the wall, push backwards over the L shoulder to return to face the wall. Work to ensure that the force of your arm pushing against the wall doesn't cause the torso/legs/shoulders to become misaligned. Repeat. Repeat again except when your back is against the wall, instead of turning back the way you came, continue the circle, pressing with your L hand and turning backwards over your R shoulder. Repeat. Repeat entire exercise beginning on the left side.

 VIDEO REFERENCE 4.1. *Knee Turns*

Straight Leg Turns

Using the same preparation position and alignment as the knee turns, begin in an L position with legs straight out on the wall (90 degrees). Gently release the feet from the wall as you complete a half turn backwards over your R shoulder so that you end with your back against the wall and legs outstretched. (This exercise requires a very strong psoas and abdominals so, unless students are very strong, work up to this.) Using your R hand against the wall both pushing away and turning the body, return over your L shoulder to your starting L position facing the wall. Repeat. Repeat again except when your back is against the wall, instead of turning back the way you came, continue the circle, using your L hand and turning backwards over your R shoulder. Repeat. Repeat entire exercise beginning on the left side.

 VIDEO REFERENCE 4.2 *Straight Leg Turns*

Ball Turn

Turning in a ball shape takes a bit of power as the dancer needs to turn 180 degrees without the aid of swinging or momentum of any kind. This exercise begins with a deep plié in first position and then a push off the wall. This push needs to not only be directly out and away from the wall, but also work as a means to turn the dancer. Therefore, the push must be a powerful kick away from the wall and it must be angled for turning. The best way to do this is to apply push away power with both legs in addition to torque from the inside leg. (If you are turning over your right shoulder, you would create torque using your left leg.) Once you push away, immediately draw the knees into the chest and reach around to grab knees with your arms. As you turn, release the legs so that they land on the wall. This can be repeated to the same side or sides can be alternated. (Alternating sides is a bit more difficult.)

 VIDEO REFERENCE 4.3. *Ball Turn*

Pencil Turn

Begin in the L position, grab onto the rope at eye level, plié very deeply and push away from the wall keeping your chest up. As you push away pull yourself towards the rope. At the same time lower your legs and pelvis so that your body is parallel to the wall, making as straight a line as possible. Push forward against the harness with your pelvis to achieve a flat shape. As your body is gaining distance from the wall, turn. As you finish the turn, bring the legs back up to the wall to land in an L position. If students have trouble completing the turn, I add to the sequence a few pushes away from the wall without turning to help them build strength and momemtum. The sequence I use is: plié and push away from wall in L position without turning 3×, pencil turn over right shoulder and land. Repeat 4×. Repeat entire exercise turning over left shoulder.

Intermediate: Plié and push away 1× and then turn. Repeat 4×. Repeat turning to the other side.

Advanced: Plié and pencil turn, alternating sides. Repeat 8×.

 VIDEO REFERENCE 4.4. *Pencil Turn*

Attitude Turn

This is a 180 degree turn in place with one leg in 'attitude'. This turn requires a bit of strength because there isn't any momentum to help you get around. You have to rely on the power of your legs. The turn originates from the L position. From L, step onto your inside foot (the foot that is not leading in the direction you are swinging) on the wall and push off. (For students who are having trouble turning with enough force, stepping with the inside leg behind the outside leg – as you would in a grapevine – prior to pushing off gives them a bit of extra power.) This push needs to not be directly out and away from the wall, but rather is a combination of push from the wall and torque for turning. Once you push, elongate the outside leg. Straighten and point the toe. This leg leads the turn out and around. The legs are apart (in as wide a V as possible) and the knee of the secondary leg is bent 90 degrees and is in parallel so that the foot points directly down to the ground. (Not a true attitude, but you get the derivation.) Toes are pointed. The elongated leg lands on the wall on the other side followed by the bent leg that must extend as both feet land and plié in parallel first position. For R turns, the sequences goes: step behind R foot with L foot, push off with L foot, R leg leads the turn as L leg is in 'attitude'. Land on R leg and then L. This exercise can be repeated on the same side or can alternate sides. This exercise can be accomplished with the torso sitting up, or with the torso reaching away from the pelvis on a 45 degree angle, with the torso in plank or even with the torso hanging below the pelvis with the legs reaching up. Clearly, the changes in torso make the exercises more difficult. The lower your torso, the closer your head is to the wall, so be careful.

 VIDEO REFERENCE 4.5. *Attitude Turn*

V Turn

This is a 180 degree turn in place with legs in a V position. The turn begins in an L position. From L, plié deeply and push away from the wall with both feet with a combination of power away from the wall and torque power to turn the body. (The inside leg pushes a little harder than the outside leg to achieve the turn.) Once you push away, elongate the outside leg (the leg you are leading with) and then the inside leg as soon as it's possible. Straighten and point the toes. Your legs should create a V shape (from a bird's eye view) and your torso should be sitting tall with your ischial tuberosities reaching down to the ground. Abdominals are pressing back into the spine. The elongated leg lands on the wall of the opposite side, followed quickly by the second elongated leg. Plié deeply as you land. This exercise can be repeated on the same side or alternating sides.

 VIDEO REFERENCE 4.6. *V Turn*

L Turn

This is a 180 degree turn with the legs forming an L with the torso. The turn begins in L position. Plié deeply on both legs and push away from the wall with both feet. To aid with torque, push away a bit harder with the inside leg than you do the outside leg ("inside" and "outside" are related to the direction you are turning. If you're turning to the R, your R leg is the "outside" leg and your L leg is the "inside" leg.). This will aid in creating the half turn necessary. Once you push away, elongate both legs and put legs together. Keep legs straight and point the toes. Your body should create an L shape with your torso sitting directly up and legs directly out and together. The elongated legs land on the wall on the opposite side and end in deep plié. This exercise can be repeated on the same side or sides can alternate.

 VIDEO REFERENCE 4.7. *L Turn*

Starfish

Beginning in the L position, slowly lower into plank position. Step out to second position and raise arms to sides so that you are in the shape of an X. Plié deeply and push away from the wall, keeping the X shape. Be sure that your shoulders and ankles do not sag or hang below your pelvis. Push forward against your harness with your pelvis to ensure a flat body position. Try not to crunch in your neck. Think of elongating from the top of your head. Your neck is long and chin released to the ceiling. This can also be varied to begin in a plank and the arms and legs open to an X as the student pushes away from the wall and returns to plank (in plié) when they land. Repeat 4×. Raise to L position. Rest. Repeat.

 VIDEO REFERENCE 4.8. *Starfish*

Cartwheel

From the L position, place feet into a parallel second position and lower into a plank. Raise arms from sides so that you are in an X shape. Gently walk feet to the left so that the torso moves to the right. When the legs run out of wall, push gently in a curve and place your hands on the wall. Walk hands along the wall in the same direction. Be sure to keep the entire torso flat, pushing abdominals back. When the arms run out of wall space, push off in a curve to land on the closest foot and keep going. The motion looks like a stationary cartwheel. Repeat 4×. Return to L position. Rest. Lower down into plank. Repeat entire exercise in the opposite direction. Return to L position.

Intermediate: Remove the rest in between sides. Rest. Repeat.

Advanced: Remove the rest in between sides and repeat 8× per side. Rest. Repeat.

 VIDEO REFERENCE 4.9. *Cartwheel*

Torso Flip

From the L position, feet in parallel, slowly lower to a plank position. Lift the right leg off the wall and keeping it straight, raise it towards the ceiling. Pivot on your standing leg and shift your torso so that you are facing the floor. The raised leg moves up and over the rope holding you. Your grigri and carabiners will shift underneath you. (Be careful you don't pinch any soft parts in the pelvis region.) The other foot should remain firmly on the wall. Keep shifting over until the R foot comes in contact with the wall. At this point you should be in an inverted L position with both feet firmly on the wall and the harness and rope between your legs. Hold. Reverse this movement, lifting the R leg up off the wall and toward your chest, pivot on your standing leg, shift your pelvis and torso so you come back to a plank position. Repeat 2×. Return to L position. Rest. Repeat except once inverted, instead of lifting the same leg you just placed on the wall to go back over the rope in the direction that you came from, lift the opposite leg and flip your torso back to plank, thus finishing the circle. Repeat 2×. Return to L position. Repeat entire exercise beginning on the L side.

 VIDEO REFERENCE 4.10. *Torso Flip*

Pommel Horse

(So named by one of my students who discovered this awesomeness while improvising in class.)

Begin in an L position. Walk your feet down the wall and allow your chest to rise towards the rope and the wall. Keep your body as upright as possible as if you were standing on the ground. Using quite a bit of force, swing your head and torso to the R, keeping your body in plank, your legs will rise up between the rope and the wall and swing in an arc. Your head and chest move downwards as the legs move up. Keep the arc going and your legs will swing down the other side as chest and head rises. As they lower towards the ground, use the momentum to swing them back up again and repeat. Use your hands on the wall as needed. The legs should make complete circles. Repeat. On last circle, end with legs lowered. Walk up the wall to an L position. Rest. Repeat to the other side. (This requires strong abdominals so you may not want to use it until your students are strong enough.)

 VIDEO REFERENCE 4.11. *Pommel Horse*

Backbend

Begin in the L position, lower down into plank. Walk down the wall a few steps until the knees are against the wall and legs are hanging. At the same time, release in your upper back, allowing your shoulders to drop down to the floor. Hold. Tuck your toes under and push against the wall to hop back up to the plank position. Repeat 4×.

 VIDEO REFERENCE 4.12 *Backbend*

Turning Backbend

Begin in the L position, lower down into plank. Walk down the wall a few steps until the knees are against the wall and legs are hanging. At the same time, release in your upper back, allowing your shoulders to drop to the floor. Hold. Tuck your L toe under and push against the wall to spin a half turn backwards over your right shoulder so that your face is towards the wall. Use your hands to catch yourself. Use your hands to push away and spin back the way you came (backwards over your left shoulder). Walk up the wall to plank. Raise to the L position. Repeat. Repeat entire exercise except once your face is towards the wall, use your hands to keep pushing in the same direction (backwards over your right shoulder), thus completing the circle. Walk up the wall to plank. Raise to L position. Repeat.

 VIDEO REFERENCE 4.13. *Turning Backbend*

Backbend to Pushup

Begin in the L position, lower down into plank. Walk down the wall a few steps until the legs are hanging against the wall and, at the same time, release your upper back, allowing your shoulders to drop to the floor. Hold. Tuck your L toe under and push against the wall to spin backwards over your right shoulder so that your face is to the wall. Use your hands, palms against the wall, to catch yourself, placing them a little above head height. Pull your knees into your chest. Straighten your arms and flatten the torso, pressing your abdominals into your harness. Hold. Release arms and legs back down. Use your hands to push away and spin back the way you came. Walk up the wall to plank. Repeat entire exercise. When planked, rise to the L position. Rest. Repeat entire exercise except after you complete the push up, use your hands to keep pushing in the same direction (backwards over your right shoulder), thus completing the circle. Walk up the wall to plank. Repeat. Finish in plank position and then rise to L position.

Intermediate: instead of pulling knees into the chest, pull in one knee and extend the other. Alternate the leg that is extended.

Advanced: Instead of pulling knees into the chest, extend the legs straight out.

 VIDEO REFERENCE 4.14. *Backbend to Pushup*

Inverted Spin

From L position, drop down to a plank position. Walk your legs up the wall while bending in the knees to invert. Allow the back of the body to touch the wall and wrap legs around the rope. Open arms to the high diagonal (hands are on either side of torso), palms flat against the wall. Push your pelvis against the harness to ensure a full body alignment. Using your hands, push to complete half turn by turning backwards over your right shoulder. Use hands on the wall to stop the spin when you are facing the wall. Using your hands to push turn back the way you came (backwardsover your left shoulder). Repeat. Repeat entire exercise except when facing the wall, complete the circle by pushing with your hands to complete the turn backwards (over your right shoulder). Repeat. Unhook legs from rope and walk down the wall back to the plank position. Come up to the L position. Rest. Go back down into the plank position. Repeat entire exercise on the right side. Unhook legs from rope and walk down the wall back to the plank position. Come up to the L position.

Intermediate: Remove coming back to plank and L position between sets. Remain inverted for the duration of the exercise.

Advanced: Complete full turns instead of half turns, repeating each set 4×.

 VIDEO REFERENCE 4.15. *Inverted Spin*

Inverted Attitude

From L position, walk your legs up the wall while bending in the knees to invert. Allow the back of the body to touch the wall and wrap legs around the rope. Open arms to the low diagonal, palms flat against the wall. Push your pelvis against the harness to ensure a full body alignment. Using your hands, push to half turn backwards over your right shoulder. Use hands on the wall to stop the turn so you end facing the wall. Release your R leg from the rope and open it out to the back into attitude. Push away from the wall with your hands and return to the wall. Repeat 4×. Replace leg on rope. Using your hands, push to turn back the way you came (backwards over left shoulder). Unhook legs from rope and walk down the wall back to the plank position. Come back to plank position and up to the L position. Rest. Go back down into the plank position. Repeat entire exercise turning backwards over your left shoulder and releasing the L leg from the rope into a back attitude.

Intermediate: Remove coming back to plank and L position between sets. Remain inverted for the duration of the exercise. Push away from the wall harder to get body way out into space. Add extra counts for this.

Advanced: work with varying tempos, both slow and fast.

 VIDEO REFERENCE 4.16. *Inverted Attitude*

Turning Inverted Attitude

From L position, walk your legs up the wall while bending in the knees to invert. Allow the back of the body to touch the wall and wrap legs around the rope. Open arms to the low diagonal, palms flat against the wall. Push your pelvis against the harness to ensure a full body alignment. Using your hands, push to complete half turn backwards over your right shoulder. Use hands on the wall to stop the turn so you are facing the wall. Release your R leg from the rope and open it out to the back into attitude. Push away from the wall with your hands while, at the same time, pushing on an angle with the inside hand so that you generate torque and your body completes a full turn to the left. Return to the wall with a plié in the elbows. Repeat 4×. Replace leg on rope. Using your hands, push to turn back the way you came (backwards over left shoulder). Unhook legs from rope and walk down the wall back to the plank position. Come up to the L position. Rest. Go back down into the plank position. Repeat entire exercise turning backwards over your left shoulder and releasing your L leg from the rope into back attitude.

Intermediate: Remove coming back to plank and L position between sets. Remain inverted for the duration of the exercise. Push away from the wall harder to get body way out into space. Add extra counts for this.

Advanced: Drop both legs into attitude back. This requires particular attention to the alignment of the abdominals and shoulders in the inverted position.

 VIDEO REFERENCE 4.17. *Turning Inverted Attitude*

Sideways Swinging Backbends

From L position, take a few steps down the wall and bend your knees until you are sitting with knees against the wall. Back is long, head reaching up. Be sure that your knees are parallel to your hips and are together. Gently push to move your body position slightly (45 degrees) so that your right shoulder and hip are touching the wall. This is the preparation position for this exercise. Release your back and hips and allow your body to back bend with the right shoulder and hip touching the wall. Using your right hand at hip or lower level, push away and spin so that the body completes a half turn. The head should go away from the wall. Use the left hand to control the ending of the turn. Use the left hand to push the body back in the direction that it came from, head toward the wall. Repeat 4×. Repeat exercise but this time, turn so that the head moves toward the wall. This will require more strength for pushing and rotation of the body. Push back in the direction that you came from. Repeat 4×. Pull body up to sitting position with the right side of the body against the wall. Back is long, knees are the same height as the pelvis, ankles are directly below knees and legs are together. Turn slightly so that knees are against the wall. Walk legs back to L position.

Intermediate: Do the same exercise except instead of a back bend, the body should be in partial plank with knees together and bent and feet dropping down to the floor.

Advanced: Do the same exercise except instead of a back bend, the body should be in a full plank.

 VIDEO REFERENCE 4.18. *Sideways Swinging Backbends*

Sideways Swinging Backbends with Plank

From L position, walk your feet down until you are sitting with knees against the wall. Knees should be the same height as the pelvis. Gently push to move your body position slightly so that your right shoulder and hip are touching the wall. Release your back and pelvis and allow your body to plank with the right side of the body touching the wall. Hold. Drop into back bend. Using your right hand at hip or lower level, push away from the wall so that the body completes a half turn. The head should go away from the wall. Use the left hand to control the landing of the turn. Raise up to plank. Hold. Release back into back bend. Push head away from wall to complete half turn. Rise up to plank. Hold. Repeat 2× more. After last plank, rise up to sitting position. Turn slightly to face wall. Walk up to L position. Rest. Repeat entire phrase except use the right hand and push the head toward the wall. This will require more strength for pushing and rotation of body. Repeat 4× total, pushing head toward the wall for each half turn. After final plank, pull body up to sitting position with the right side of the body against the wall. Turn slightly so that knees are against the wall. Walk legs back to L position. Repeat entire phrase beginning on the left side.

Intermediate: After raising up to plank include: hold, pull legs in to the chest, hold, release them back to plank, hold. Continue with exercise. When pulling legs into chest, keep torso in plank position and arms at sides.

Advanced: Following the intermediate directions, alter the half turns so that, instead of going back from where they came on the repeat, keep going in the same direction to complete the turn.

 VIDEO REFERENCE 4.19. *Sideways Swinging Backbends with Plank*

Turning Plank Handstand

From the L position, lower down into plank. Plié and gently push off from the wall, turning towards your R in a half turn. Keep torso flat but, as you turn, pull in knees to your chest. (This takes pressure off the abdominals.) Land on your hands with your head toward the wall, arms straight and extend body into plank. Plié the arms and pull the legs into the chest and gently push off the wall, turning back the way you came (to the left). Extend legs as your feet return to the wall. Repeat 2×. Repeat exercise except after the push up, instead of turning back the way you came, keep going in the same direction (to the right) to complete the circle. Repeat 2×. Return to L position. Rest. Lower down to plank. Repeat the entire exercise to the left.

Intermediate: Remove the rest between sides. Vary the tempo, gradually increasing the speed of the turn and the time between turn.

Advanced: As you push off the wall, do not pull legs into torso. Allow legs to straighten. Be sure that ankles and shoulders do not sag downwards. Keep legs straight the entire exercise, allowing a plié when taking off from and returning to the wall.

 VIDEO REFERENCE 4.20. *Turning Plank Handstand*

Turning T Handstand

From the L position, lower down into plank. Turn entire body to face the right. Shift harness so that the carabiner is at your left hip. Your body should create a "T" with the wall. Place feet in parallel first position and deeply bend knees. Push off the wall and turn forward a half turn until your hands are on the wall. Your body should be planked on its side. Plié arms and turn back the way you came. (Pike slightly at the waist, feet lead the way back to the wall.) Repeat 2×. Repeat except instead of going back the way you came, complete the circle by continuing forward motion of the feet (like a handspring) and land. Repeat 2×. Turn body back to plank position, shifting harness back to center. Raise to the L position. Rest. Repeat entire exercise, turning the body to face the left and shifting harness to the right hip.

Intermediate: Remove the rest between sides. Repeat.

Advanced: Vary the tempo, gradually increasing the speed of the turn and the time between turns.

 VIDEO REFERENCE 4.21. *Turning T*

Supported Somersault (front and back)

From the L position, lower down into plank. Turn entire body to face the right. Shift harness so that the carabiner is at your left hip. Your body should create a "T" with the wall. Raise your left arm to full extension and grab onto the rope. Your arm should create a triangle shape with your body and the rope. Be careful of contracting the arm muscles and pulling your torso out of alignment. Place feet in parallel first position. Plié. Push away from the wall while tucking your head and your knees into your chest. Grab onto your knees with your free hand. Fully rotate the body, landing on your feet in plié and extending your head and torso out to side plank again. Focus on using only the force necessary to complete the objective. Motion should be gentle with a soft landing at the end. Watch your balance. Repeat 4×. Shift back to plank, making sure that the center part of your harness is at your belly button. Come up to L position. Rest. Repeat entire exercise to the left side. Shift back to plank, making sure that the center part of your harness is at your belly button. Come up to L position. Rest. Repeat entire exercise, somersaulting backwards. Going backwards is a little scarier than forwards because you can't see where you're going. I encourage students to tuck their heads tightly and to use a little more force when pushing off the wall until they get a feel for how much force is needed. I also spot them to prevent any potential safety concerns by grabbing onto the back of their harness and walking them in a circle. Once they feel the motion, it's easier for them to replicate it. Keep the ball tight when turning backwards, especially in the neck/head to prevent potential injury.

Intermediate: Vary the tempo of the spins. Shorten time spent rebalancing and reorienting before/after flip.

Advanced: Remove your upper arm from the rope. Somersault without holding on to the rope keeping body aligned properly.

 VIDEO REFERENCE 4.22. *Supported Somersault*

Supported Front Walkover

From the L position, lower down into plank. Turn entire body to face the right. Shift harness so that the carabiner is at your left hip. Your body should create a 'T' with the wall. Raise your left arm to full extension and grab onto the rope. Your arm should create a triangle shape with your body and the rope. Be careful of contracting the arm muscles and pulling your torso out of alignment. Place the feet in parallel fifth position, left foot front. Plié. Push away from the wall one foot at a time, leading with the left leg as it slides through to the back. Be sure that legs are in a V shape (from a bird's eye view), keeping torso open. Turn forwards using the outstretched free hand to push through the wall. Keep going around, finishing the 360 degree turn and land one foot at a time to come back to the T position. Focus on using only the force necessary to complete the objective. Motion should be gentle and shouldn't fly far away from the wall with a soft landing at the end. Watch your balance. Repeat 4×. Shift back to plank, making sure that the center part of your harness is at your belly button. Come up to L position. Rest. Repeat entire exercise on the left side, making sure the right foot is front in parallel fifth and you begin the walkover with your right foot as it slides back and leads the exercise. Shift back to plank, making sure that the center part of your harness is at your belly button. Come up to L position. Rest.

Intermediate: Vary the tempo of the walkover. Shorten time spent rebalancing and reorienting before and after. Alternate left and right sides.

Advanced: Remove your upper arm from the rope. This requires very strong abdominals, back and torso. Alignment is very important. Do not let your head and shoulders drop below your pelvis.

 VIDEO REFERENCE 4.23. *Supported Front Walkover*

Supported Front Flip

This is a variation of the supported front walkover where, during the inversion, the legs are straight and are together. Keep your torso straight. Do not bend at the waist. (Depending on your rig, this may require a higher vertical surface with longer rope to be successful.) From the L position, lower down into plank. Turn entire body to face the right. Shift harness so that the carabiner is at your left hip. Your body should create a 'T' with the wall. Raise your left arm to full extension and grab onto the rope. Your arm should create a triangle shape with your body and the rope. Be careful of contracting the arm muscles and pulling your torso out of alignment. Place the feet in parallel first position. Plié. Push away from the wall keeping legs straight. Turn forwards brushing through the wall with the outstretched free hand. (The hand can be removed once the student is confident.) Push through and away and land on both feet to come back to the T position. Focus on using only the force necessary to complete the objective. Watch your balance. Repeat 4×. Shift back to plank, making sure that the center part of your harness is at your belly button. Come up to L position. Rest. Repeat entire exercise on the left side, making sure feet are in parallel first. Shift back to plank, making sure that the center part of your harness is at your belly button. Come up to L position. Rest.

Intermediate: Vary the tempo of the flip. Shorten time spent rebalancing and reorienting before and after the flip. Alternate right and left sides.

Advanced: Remove your upper arm from the rope. This is very complex and requires very strong abdominals, torso, back muscles and proper alignment. Do not allow your head and shoulders to drop below your pelvis.

 VIDEO REFERENCE 4.24. *Supported Front Flip*

Supported Back Walkover

I separate the back from the front walkovers because, although it's just a reversal of the original, there are very different muscle contractions and elongations that occur and a different type of coordination is required. The back flip is a little scarier because you will need to lead with your head and arm and you can't really see where you're going, I sometimes encourage students to slowly flip backwards in a little ball with outstretched arm until they understand how the backward motion will feel. In this way, they learn the appropriate amount of push needed to clear the wall. I spot all students new to flipping to ensure that no safety hazards occur by grabbing onto the back of their harness and walking them in the path of the walkover. Once they feel the motion, it's easier for them to replicate it. There have been a few instances where students have moved immediately to two hands on the wall because, although it is more difficult and requires more strength, it makes them feel safer. In these cases, their form was unbalanced and misaligned until they gained the necessary strength to do it properly, but because they felt safe practicing, they eventually gained the tools necessary for precision and accuracy. I don't recommend this but, in some cases, it's the only option that is successful. For the supported back flip, lower to the L position, then lower down into plank. Turn entire body to face the right. Shift harness so that the carabiner is at your left hip. Your body should create a 'T' with the wall. Raise your left arm to full extension and grab onto the rope. Be careful of contracting the arm muscles and pulling your torso out of alignment. Your arm should create a right triangle shape with your body and the rope. Place the feet in parallel fifth position, left foot front. Plié. Push away from the wall one foot at a time, leading with the left leg. Be sure that legs are in a V shape (from a bird's eye view), keeping torso open and long. Use enough force and spin to clear your head so it doesn't hit the wall. Spin backwards landing on the wall on the outstretched free hand. Push through and away and land one foot at a time to come back to the T position. Focus on using only the force necessary to complete the objective. Motion should be gentle and shouldn't fly far away from the wall with a soft landing at the end. Watch your balance. Repeat 4×. Shift back to plank, making sure that the center part of your harness is at your belly button. Come up to L position. Rest. Repeat entire exercise to the left side, making sure the right foot is front in parallel fifth and you begin the flip with your right foot as it slides back. Shift back to plank, making sure that the center part of your harness is at your belly button. Come up to L position. Rest.

Intermediate: Vary the tempo of the turns. Shorten time spent rebalancing and reorienting before and after walkovers. Alternate right and left sides.

Advanced: Remove your upper arm from the rope. This requires great strength and an advanced understanding of alignment.

 VIDEO REFERENCE 4.25. *Supported Back Walkover*

Supported Back Flip

This is a variation of the supported back walkover where, during the inversion, the legs are straight and are together. Keep your torso straight. Do not bend at the waist. (Depending on your rig, this may require a higher vertical surface with longer rope to be successful.) From the L position, lower down into plank. Turn entire body to face the right. Shift harness so that the carabiner is at your left hip. Your body should create a 'T' with the wall. Raise your left arm to full extension and grab onto the rope. Your arm should create a triangle shape with your body and the rope. Be careful of contracting the arm muscles and pulling your torso out of alignment. Place the feet in parallel first position. Plié. Push away from the wall keeping legs straight. Turn backwards landing on the wall on the outstretched free hand. (Once students are comfortable, the arm can be removed.) Push through and away and land on both feet to come back to the T position. Focus on using only the force necessary to complete the objective. Watch your balance. Repeat 4×. Shift back to plank, making sure that the center part of your harness is at your belly button. Come up to L position. Rest. Repeat entire exercise on the left side, making sure feet are in parallel first position. Shift back to plank, making sure that the center part of your harness is at your belly button. Come up to L position. Rest.

Intermediate: Vary the tempo of the flip. Shorten time spent rebalancing and reorienting before and after the flip. Alternate right and left sides.

Advanced: Remove your upper arm from the rope. This requires advanced muscular development and understanding of anatomical alignment.

 VIDEO REFERENCE 4.26. *Supported Back Flip*

Somersault Walkover Combo

Using the information in the above two exercises, I created a third that pairs them. Once balance and coordination is achieved for each exercise individually, this challenges the aerialist to work with coordination among diverse movements, force and dynamic pulls. This combination pairs the forward somersault and the backward flip together with the backward somersault and forward flip. As students progress, I recommend pairing any of the movements in this section together to create new exercises or longer chains to make phrases. Transitioning from one element to the other is great experience for more advanced work. From the L position, lower down into plank. Turn entire body to face the right. Shift harness so that the carabiner is at your left hip. Your body should create a "T" with the wall. Raise your left arm to full extension and grab onto the rope. Place the feet in parallel first position. Plié. Forward somersault, land and immediately take off in backward walkover, land. Repeat 2×. Backward somersault, land and immediately take off in forward walkover, land. Repeat 2×. Forward somersault, land and immediately take off in forward walkover, land. Repeat 2×. Backward somersault, land and immediately take off in backward walkover, land. Repeat 2×. Shift back to plank, making sure that the center part of your harness is at your belly button. Come up to L position. Rest. Repeat entire exercise to the left side.

Intermediate: Vary the tempo of the spins. Shorten time spent rebalancing and reorienting before/after walkover.

Advanced: Remove your upper arm from the rope. Walkover without holding onto anything. Use both hands on the wall as you turn until proficient.

 VIDEO REFERENCE 4.27. *Somersault Walkover Combo*

CHAPTER 5

Across the Floor

Motion and Agility

In this portion of the class, we begin to move away from the wall through pushes, jumps and spins. For most of my students, this is the *fun* part. It's true that one of the joys of aerial dance is the feeling of flight. The joy comes from an awareness of freedom from earthbound forces (sort of) and the ability to move in new ways not possible when grounded. Part of what makes this portion of class enjoyable is the hang time. Moving from the end of a forty foot rope can feel the way one might imagine astronauts feel on the moon. As if there is a

Figure 5.01 Agility in motion
Credit: © Washington and Lee University 2011

world of time between pushing away from a surface and returning. In aerial dance, all sorts of movement can fit into that world and give the appearance of weightlessness and timelessness. For someone used to the rigors of traditional dance, fun is an apt word.

For this portion of the class, the dancer is asked to lower her/himself to the bottom sector or just above the bottom third of the wall. This lengthening of the rope gives more freedom to the dancer but also requires a great deal of control. In this vertical surface area, the dancer no longer feels glued to the wall. In fact, a connection is tenuous at best. Planking generally results in feet slipping down from the wall. Maintaining this position at this height requires greater muscular strength and a more complete understanding of the body in space. Balance becomes challenging and force and timing, which the aerialist may now feel she's conquered through the middle sectors exercises, have changed. The beauty of this zone is that airtime is increased. It takes less force to gain more time away from the wall. Spins can now be doubled and tripled before returning to the wall and fleeting motions can be expounded upon.

Some of the exercises in this portion of the class are similar to previous work and are included here as a further challenge to equilibrium and balance. These exercises give the dancer a greater freedom to explore diagonal space, including arms more fully into the movement and coordinating movements with timing and with force. In a traditional dance class, this may be when the teacher calls dancers to "move across the floor". The body you've

Figure 5.02 Abdominal strength is key for control at any height
Credit: © Washington and Lee University 2009

warmed up, worked through technical exercises and muscle building activities, and challenged in the freer place of center is now ready to begin the large movement portion of the class. This is the culmination of all the previous work. In short, you begin to feel as if you are really dancing.

The order I outline below is generally what I use in class. I don't always use all of them. When I teach intensively, five days a week, I tend to alternate exercises with days so that the students' bodies aren't too taxed. Therefore, the order can be switched up. After spending a little time with these exercises, the descriptions may start to seem a bit pedantic, however, as with all of the exercises so far, I've tried to be as specific as I can in each description, even if the movements are similar. I am assuming that the reader won't necessarily use all of them but may pick and choose. For that reason, I want to be very clear.

Swings

From the L position, arms at your sides reaching down into the ground, push with your right foot to put yourself in motion swinging to the left. When arriving to the left, push with greater force to swing yourself further to the right. Continue back and forth and make the pendulum increase in size and scope. Practice pushing to gain in length of the swing from side to side. Practice pushing to gain depth away from the wall. Legs should be straight and in a V position when swinging. Do not allow your legs to fall below your pelvis on the swing. Use your psoas and your abdominals. Sit tall in your harness. Do not allow the pressure on your legs to force your torso to slump.

Intermediate: Arms in second position.

Advanced: Arms in fifth position.

 VIDEO REFERENCE 5.1. *Swings*

Swings with Ball Turn

Using the swings as a means to ball turn, take a little time to gradually build up the swings left to right. When sufficient swing is achieved, add a ball turn in one direction. To do this, at the height of the swing, place both feet together on the wall and push off. This push needs to not be directly out and away from the wall, but rather as a means to spin the dancer in a half circle. Therefore, the push must be at the highest point of the swing and it must be angled for torque. Once you push away, immediately draw the knees into the chest and reach around to grab knees. You will turn as you swing to the opposite side. When you've reached the maximum swing of the pendulum to the opposite side, release the legs. Push one foot against the wall to resume flat swings. The exercise I give is: Swing RLR, on the swing to the right land on both feet and push against the wall with both feet and turn/swing to left. Upon landing on left side, push off with left foot only to flat swing to the right and repeat the exercise. After performing this turn 4× to the right, switch to the left. This can be accomplished by swinging 1× between sets. In this way, after the fourth swing, you push away from the left side with both legs and land on the right. Repeat 4×. If you wish to repeat the entire exercise, simply swing 1× between sets.

Intermediate: Repeat exercise with arms in second position. Repeat the entire exercise but remove all swings except the swing to change sides. The combination would be swing R, ball turn L, ball turn R, ball turn L. Repeat 4×. Repeat on other side.

Advanced: Repeat exercise with arms in fifth position. Body should be tall reaching up through the head and down through the ischial tuberocities. Repeat the entire exercise but remove all swings except the swing to change sides. The combination would be swing R, ball turn L, ball turn R, ball turn L. Repeat 4×. Repeat on other side.

 VIDEO REFERENCE 5.2. *Swings with Ball Turn*

Swings with Attitude Turn

Using the swings as a means to attitude turn, take a little time to gradually build up the swings left to right. When sufficient swing is achieved, add an attitude turn in one direction. To do this, at the height of the swing, place the inside foot (the foot that is not leading in the direction you are swinging) on the wall and push off. This push needs to not be directly out and away from the wall, but rather as a means to spin the dancer in a half circle. Therefore, the push must be at the highest point of the swing and it must be angled to produce torque. Once you push away, elongate the leading leg. Straighten and point the toe. This leg leads the turn out and away from the wall. The knee of the secondary leg is bent 90 degrees at the knee and in parallel so the foot points downward. (Again, not a true attitude but a derivation thereof.) The elongated leg lands on the wall at the height of the pendulum swing to the opposite side. Place second foot on the wall and push off the second foot to begin the flat swing again. The sequence I use is: Swing RLR, on the swing to the right land on both feet and push against the wall with left foot and turn while swinging to left. Elongate right leg, straighten knee and point toe. Land on left side with the right leg and quickly add second leg. Push off with the left leg to go back to flat swings. After performing this 4× to the right, switch to the left. This can be accomplished by swinging 1× extra, side to side between sets.

Intermediate: Arms begin low circling the rope in front of you near your carabiner and move into second position as the leg is extended. Repeat 4×. Swing to change sides. Repeat 4×. Repeat entire exercise, with one swing to begin and with no swings between turns.

Advanced: Repeat entire intermediate exercise adding an extension of the torso back 45 degrees in the harness away from the leg that is extended, bringing torso back up as the leg hits the wall. This change in back position is similar to the change in torso movement between L position and plank. Abdominals and lower back are engaged and face and chest is raised to the ceiling. Circle arms around rope at carabiner height and open them out to second position as you turn and as your torso releases. Repeat 4×. Swing once to change sides. Repeat 4×. Repeat entire exercise with one swing to begin and then no swings between turns.

 VIDEO REFERENCE 5.3. *Swings with Attitude Turn*

Swings with V Turn

This combination uses the swings as a means to V turn. When sufficient swing is achieved, add a double arabesque spin in one direction. To do this, at the height of the swing, place both feet on the wall and push off. This push needs to not be directly out and away from the wall, but rather as a means to turn the dancer in a half circle. Therefore, the push must be at the highest point of the swing and it must be angled for torque. The inside leg pushes a little harder than the outside leg to achieve the turn. Once you push away, elongate the outside leg (the leg you are leading with) and then the inside leg. Straighten and point the toes. Your legs should create a V shape and your torso should be sitting directly up. The elongated legs land on the wall at the height of the pendulum swing to the opposite side. As you place the second foot on the wall, push off that foot to begin the flat swing again. The sequence I use is: Swing RLR, on the swing to the right land on both feet and push against the wall turn and swing to left (backward over your right shoulder). Elongate the legs, straighten knees and point toes. Land on left side with the leading leg and quickly add second leg. Push off left leg to go back to flat swings, to repeat the exercise. After performing this combination 4× to the right, switch to the left. This can be accomplished by swinging 1× to the side between sets. Repeat 4×. If you wish to repeat the entire exercise, simply swing 1× between sets.

Intermediate: Repeat with arms moving from first to second position on the turn and coming back to first on the wall landing and the swings. Repeat 4× to each side. Repeat entire exercise with 45 degree back extension. Repeat entire exercise, with one swing to begin and with no swings between turns 8×.

Advanced: Repeat with arms moving from second to fifth position on the turn and coming back to second on the wall landing and for the swings. Repeat 4× on the other side. Repeat entire exercise with full back extension (90 degrees or plank). Repeat entire exercise, with one swing to begin and with no swings between turns 8×.

 VIDEO REFERENCE 5.4. *Swings with V Turn*

Swings with L Turn

This combination uses swings as a means to a closed double arabesque turn or L turn. To do this, at the height of the swing, place both feet on the wall and push off. This push needs to not be directly out and away from the wall, but rather as a means to turn the dancer in a halt circle. Therefore, the push must be at the highest point of the swing and the inside leg must push harder than the outside leg to achieve turning motion. Once you push away, elongate both legs and place legs together. Straighten and point the toes. Your body should create an L shape with your torso sitting straight up and legs directly out and together. The elongated legs land on the wall at the height of the pendulum swing to the opposite side. As you place the feet on the wall, push off (mostly with the outside leg) to begin the flat swing again. The sequence I use is: Swing RLR, on the swing to the right land on both feet and push against the wall, turn and swing to left (backward over your right shoulder). Elongate the legs, straighten knees and point toes. Land on left side with both legs. Push off with left leg to go back to flat swings and repeat the exercise. After performing this spin 4× to the right, switch to the left. This can be accomplished by swinging 1× side to side between sets.

Intermediate: Instead of three swings between spins, swing once and then spin. Repeat 4× with arms moving from first to second position on the turn and coming back to first on the wall landing. Repeat 4× on the other side.

Advanced: Instead of three swings between spins, swing once and then spin. Repeat 4× with arms moving from second to fifth position on the turn and coming back to second on the wall landing. Repeat 4× on the other side.

 VIDEO REFERENCE 5.5. *Swings with L Turn*

Swings with Spin

I place this exercise here because it naturally builds on the preceding exercises, however it is much more advanced. Depending on the level of your students, you may want to skip it and come back to it later. This exercises use swings as a means to spin turn. It's important to note that a spin turn is not a completed turn of your body, it's a complete circle around the rope. Up to this point we've been turning 360 degrees. This turn is twice that. To accomplish this, at the height of the swing place both feet on the wall and push off. This push needs to not be directly out and away from the wall, but rather as a means to turn the dancer in a full circle. Therefore, the push must be at the highest point of the swing and it must be angled. The inside leg pushes a little harder than the outside leg to achieve the turn. As you push away, grasp on to the rope with both hands at eye level and pull yourself toward the rope. Contract with your legs and torso to make your body into a small ball. You should spin in a complete circle around the rope to which you are attached at the same time that you are swinging from one side to the other. This takes practice, as timing and force are essential components that have to be given in appropriate measure. The sequence I use is: swing LRL (because this movement requires great strength and timing I start on the left so that the first swing occurs to the right. This seems to help students understand the concept easier since most of them are right handed and footed.) Push off and spin to the R. Repeat 4×. Swing 1× to change sides. Repeat entire exercise beginning with a swing to the R. Note: There is a difference between a "spin" and a "turn". For a description, see Appendix C, Terminology, pp. 169–170.

Intermediate: Swing a few times to prepare and gain height and momentum. Swing one time to the side and then spin. Repeat 4× with only one swing between spins. Swing 1× to change over between sets. Repeat.

Advanced: Swing a few times to prepare and gain height and momentum. One swing and plié deeply and spin. Upon landing, immediately plié and spin to the other side. Repeat 4×. Swing 1× to change over between sets. Repeat.

 VIDEO REFERENCE 5.6. *Swings with Spin*

Swings with Pencil Turn

Gradually build up the swings side to side. When sufficient swing is achieved, add a pencil turn in one direction. To do this, at the height of the swing, place both feet on the wall and push off. This push needs to not be directly out and away from the wall, but rather a means to turn the dancer in a circle. Therefore, the push must be at the highest point of the swing and it must be angled. The inside leg pushes a little harder than the outside leg to achieve the turn. As you push away, grasp on to the rope with both hands at face level and pull yourself up and toward the rope. At the same time lower your legs and push your pelvis forward so that your body is parallel to the wall, making as straight a line as possible. Push forward against the harness with your pelvis and backward against the harness with your legs, to achieve a flat shape. The sequence I use is: swing RLR, pencil turn backward over right shoulder and land. Repeat 4×. Repeat entire exercise turning over left shoulder after one extra swing to change sides.

Intermediate: Swing R and then pencil turn to L. Repeat 4×. Repeat to the other side.

Advanced: Swing R, pencil turn to L, pencil turn R, pencil turn L. Repeat 4×. Swing once to change sides. Repeat to the L.

 VIDEO REFERENCE 5.7. *Swings with Pencil Turn*

Swings with Cartwheel

Usually I begin exercises on the R side, just to keep things simple and because, generally, students feel more secure because it's their strong side. However, in this exercise, because the cartwheel is achieved after three swings, I begin on the L. That way the cartwheel first happens on the right side. The sequence I use is: swing LRL, as you begin to move back to the R, flatten your body out into a starfish position (another way to think of it is that you're moving from an L position to a plank position) while, at the same time, pushing off the wall with your inside foot to initiate the turn. Push your abdominals back into your spine, leave your neck long and shoulders relaxed but in line with your pelvis (don't drop your head and shoulders toward the ground). What will happen is that you will rotate slowly as you swing to the R. Your feet will give way to hands, which will push off the wall aiding in the turn (remember to plié in your elbows) and you will return to your feet. Pull back up into the L position. Repeat the three swings and the cartwheel 4×. Swing 1× to change sides. Repeat to the other side 4×.

Intermediate: Swing once L and cartwheel R. Repeat 4×. Swing 1× to change sides. Repeat on other side 4×.

Advanced: Swing RLRL. Cartwheel RLRL. Repeat 4×.

 VIDEO REFERENCE 5.8. *Swings with Cartwheel*

Flip Split Jump (aka *The Ninja*)

Use small pushes away from the wall as a means to the flip split jump, take a little time to gradually build up the power of the push offs. When sufficient distance from the wall is achieved, complete a flip split jump. To do this, begin in the L position, plié very deeply and push away from the wall keeping your chest up and your legs directly out from your pelvis (do not drop legs down to the ground as it makes the exercise exponentially more difficult). Grasp the rope with both hands at waist level (but above the carabiner and grigri). As you push away, drop your head and shoulders back away from the rope, extending your arms fully (while still holding the rope). Bring knees into the body and extend legs out straight over torso. When correctly executed, this position looks like the number 7, with head straight down to the ground, torso parallel to the vertical surface and legs flipped over the head. Eyes are looking at the wall opposite to the one to which you are rigged. This flip should occur when the body is at its maximum distance from the wall. Upon return, bend knees into body and flip pelvis back, use arms and abdominals to lift head and chest up and land in plié on the wall back in L position. The sequence I generally use is: Plié and push 3×, flip split. Repeat 4×. Rest. Repeat 4×.

Intermediate: Plié and push away, flip split. Repeat 8×. Rest. Repeat.

Advanced: As you push away from the wall, drop legs down to the ground and bring chest up towards the rope. When you've almost reached the farthest distance away from the wall, drop head and shoulders away from the rope and pull legs up and in to the body and flip. Be aware: this takes great strength and perfect timing. Use caution and build up to this gradually. Failure can result in very hard collisions of the head, back, pelvis, legs with the wall.

 VIDEO REFERENCE 5.9. *Flip Split Jump*

Superman

Beginning in the L position, slowly lower into plank position. Turn entire body to face the right. Shift harness so that the carabiner is at your left hip. Your body should create a "T" with the wall. Step into first position parallel and raise arms to fifth position so that you are in a side plank. Plié deeply and push away from the wall, keeping the shape. Be sure that your arms, shoulders and ankles do not sag or hang below your pelvis. Push forward against your harness with your pelvis to ensure a flat body position. Try not to crunch in your neck. Think of elongating out from the top of your head, neck long and chin released. Arms press into your ears. Repeat 4×. Switch pelvis to the left (carabiner at right hip). Repeat 4×. Rest. Repeat entire phrase.

 VIDEO REFERENCE 5.10. *Superman*

Somersault

From the L position, lower down into plank. Turn entire body to face the right. Shift harness so that the carabiner is at your left hip. Your body should create a "T" with the wall. Place feet in parallel first position. Plié. Push away from the wall while tucking your head and your knees into your chest. Do not hold onto the rope. Grab onto your knees. Fully rotate the body, landing on your feet in plié and extending your head and torso out to side plank again. Focus on using only the force necessary to complete the objective. Motion should be gentle with a soft landing at the end. Watch your balance. Repeat 4×. Shift back to plank, making sure that the center part of your harness is at your belly button. Come up to L position. Rest. Repeat entire exercise to the left side.

Intermediate: Vary the tempo of the somersaults. Shorten time spent rebalancing and reorienting before and after somersault.

Advanced: Vary the tempo of the somersaults. Raise number of repetitions per side. Alternate sides without using the hands to shift the placement of harness/carabiner.

 VIDEO REFERENCE 5.11. *Front Somersault*

Front Walkover

From the L position, lower down into plank. Turn entire body to face the right. Shift harness so that the carabiner is at your left hip. Your body should create a "T" with the wall. Do not hold on to the harness or rope. Abdominals are engaged and back is long. Place the feet in parallel fifth position, left foot front. Plié. Push away from the wall one foot at a time, leading with the left leg, which slides through to the back to lead the body. Be sure that legs are in a V shape (from a bird's eye view), keeping torso open. Spin forwards landing on the wall on the outstretched free hands. Push through and away and land one foot at a time to come back to the T position. Focus on using only the force necessary to complete the objective. Motion should be gentle and shouldn't fly far away from the wall with a soft landing at the end. Watch your balance. Repeat 4×. Shift back to plank, making sure that the center part of your harness is at your belly button. Come up to L position. Rest. Repeat entire exercise to the left side, making sure the right foot is front in parallel fifth and you begin the flip by sliding your right foot through to the back.

Intermediate: Vary the tempo of the spins. Shorten time spent rebalancing and reorienting before and after flip.

Advanced: Vary the tempo of the spins. Shorten time spent rebalancing and reorienting before and after flip. Shift R to L after each walkover without using the hands to reorient the harness/carabiner. Repeat 8×.

 VIDEO REFERENCE 5.12. *Front Walkover*

Front Flip

A variation of the front walkover where, during the inversion, the legs are straight and are together. Keep your torso straight. Do not bend at the waist. (Depending on your rig, this may require a higher vertical surface with longer rope to be successful.) From the L position, lower down into plank. Turn entire body to face the right. Shift harness so that the carabiner is at your left hip. Your body should create a "T" with the wall. Do not hold on to the harness or rope. Abdominals are engaged and back is long. Place the feet in parallel first position. Plié. Push away from the wall, both feet at the same time. Be sure that legs are in line with one another, keeping torso open. Spin forwards (outstretched free hands can feel for the wall in the beginning and, once mastered, it should be accomplished without hands). Land on both feet, plié, to come back to the T position. This exercise requires a lot of power so watch your balance on landing and your form in the air. Repeat 4×. Shift back to plank, making sure that the center part of your harness is at your belly button. Come up to L position. Rest. Repeat entire exercise to the left side.

Intermediate: Vary the tempo of the flips. Shorten time spent rebalancing and reorienting before and after flip.

Advanced: Vary the tempo of the flip. Shorten time spent rebalancing and reorienting before and after flip. Shift R to L after each flip without using the hands to reorient the harness/carabiner. Repeat 8×.

 VIDEO REFERENCE 5.13. *Front Flip*

Back Somersault

I separate out the front and back versions of this exercise (as well as the following two exercises) because, although they appear to be just the forward and backward version of the same thing, they are in fact quite different, use different muscles, are spatially divergent and necessitate different qualities and quantities of force. Plus, moving backward is just plain scary because you are leading with your head (and sometimes your arms). Because the dancers have already experienced moving backwards with support (holding on to the rope) in previous exercises, they have an idea of the motion and what it feels like to lead with your head. For those still tentative, I encourage them to get into the ball position, without holding on to anything, and then I rotate them through the path they will take so they can feel the motion. This helps to dispel some of the fear. (Remember to keep the ball tight when turning backwards, especially in the neck and head to prevent potential injury.) If I feel this is asking too much or a particular student isn't ready for it, they perform this exercise (and the following two) supported (with one arm holding onto the rope).

From the L position, lower down into plank. Turn entire body to face the right. Shift harness so that the carabiner is at your left hip. Your body should create a "T" with the wall. Place feet in parallel first position. Plié. Push away from the wall with torque to turn you backwards while tucking your head and your knees into your chest. Do not hold onto the rope. Grab onto your knees with your free hand. Fully rotate the body, landing on your feet in plié and extending your head and torso out to side plank again. Focus on using only the force necessary to complete the objective. Motion should be gentle with a soft landing at the end. Watch your balance. For those who have difficulty completing the circle, I suggest pulling the arms into the ball strongly or even circling them in to the body to create extra turning torque. Repeat 4×. Shift back to plank, making sure that the center part of your harness is at your belly button. Come up to L position. Rest. Repeat entire exercise to the left side.

Intermediate: Vary the tempo of the spins. Shorten time spent rebalancing and reorienting before and after flip.

Advanced: Vary the tempo of the spins. Shift R to L after each somersault without using the hands to reorient the harness/carabiner.

 VIDEO REFERENCE 5.14. *Back Somersault*

Back Walkover

For the back walkover lower to the L position, then lower down into plank. Turn entire body to face the right. Shift harness so that the carabiner is at your left hip. Your body should create a "T" with the wall. Hands should not be holding onto the harness or rope. Place the feet in parallel fifth position, right foot front. Plié. Push away from the wall one foot at a time, leading with the right leg. Be sure that legs are in a V shape (from a bird's eye view), keeping torso open and long. Use enough force to clear your head so it doesn't hit the wall.

Spin backwards landing on the wall on the outstretched free hands. Push through and away and land one foot at a time to come back to the T position. Focus on using only the force necessary to complete the objective. Motion should be gentle, shouldn't fly away from the wall, and should have a soft landing at the end. Watch your balance. Repeat 4×. Shift back to plank, making sure that the center part of your harness is at your belly button. Come up to L position. Rest. Repeat entire exercise to the left side, making sure the left foot is front in parallel fifth and you begin the walkover with your left foot as it slides forward.

Intermediate: Vary the tempo of the walkover. Shorten time spent rebalancing and reorienting before and after walkover.

Advanced: Vary the tempo of the walkover. Shorten time spent rebalancing and reorienting before and after walkover. Shift R to L after each walkover without using the hands to reorient the harness/carabiner. Repeat 8×.

 VIDEO REFERENCE 5.15. *Back Walkover*

Back Flip

A variation of the back walkover where, during the inversion, the legs are straight and are together. Keep your torso straight. Do not bend at the waist. This can be quite scary to introductory students so take time and work up to this. Knowing where to land and how to spin without using your eyes is a learned skill. (Depending on your rig, this may require a higher vertical surface with longer rope to be successful.) From the L position, lower down into plank. Turn entire body to face the right. Shift harness so that the carabiner is at your left hip. Your body should create a "T" with the wall. Do not hold on to the harness or rope. Abdominals are engaged and back is long. Place the feet in parallel first position. Plié. Push away from the wall, both feet at the same time. Be sure that legs are in line with one another, keeping torso open. Flip backwards (outstretched free hands can feel for the wall in the beginning and, once mastered, it should be accomplished without hands). Land on both feet, plié, come back to the T position. This exercise requires a lot of power so watch your balance on landing and your form in the air. Repeat 4×. Shift back to plank, making sure that the center part of your harness is at your belly button. Come up to L position. Rest. Repeat entire exercise to the left side.

Intermediate: Vary the tempo of the flips. Shorten time spent rebalancing and reorienting before and after flip.

Advanced: Vary the tempo of the flip. Shorten time spent rebalancing and reorienting before and after flip. Shift R to L after each flip without using the hands to reorient the harness/carabiner. Repeat 8×.

 VIDEO REFERENCE 5.16. *Back Flip*

Supported Forward Somersault to Handstand

From the L position, lower down into plank. Turn entire body to face the right. Shift harness so that the carabiner is at your left hip. Your body should create a "T" with the wall. Raise your left arm to full extension and grab onto the rope. Your arm should create a right triangle shape with your body and the rope. Place feet in parallel first position. Plié. Push away from the wall while tucking your head and your knees into your chest. Fully rotate the body, turning one and a half times, landing on your free hand with elbows in plié and extending your head and torso out straight to side plank again. (Some students find it easier to balance in the handstand by removing both hands from the rope as the somersault ends, so that is an option.) Be aware that the force you use pushing away may be different from the force you use to spin your body. Watch your balance. After balancing in the handstand, bend at the waist and bring your feet back to the wall (backwards from the direction that you just spun). Repeat 4×. I generally allow 2 counts for the spin, 2 counts for handstand and balance, 2 counts to place feet back and 2 counts to regain balance to begin again. This can be done in half time but I find that, in the early stages, movement that is too slow is just as hard as too fast. Try to find the right balance between enough speed to accomplish the task but not so much time that the muscles are straining with effort just to stay erect. Repeat 2×. Repeat the movement on this side again but, at the end of the handstand, flip onto your feet by continuing the motion of the spin with body outstretched in handstand position (in the same direction as the preceding somersault). Repeat 2×. Shift back to plank, making sure that the center part of your harness is at your belly button. Come up to L position. Rest. Repeat entire exercise to the left.

Intermediate: Vary the tempo of the exercise. Shorten the time spent rebalancing and reorienting before and after flip and lengthen time in horizontal handstand plank position.

Advanced: Remove your upper arm from the rope. Somersault and handstand without holding on to anything. Arms are around knees during somersault and on the wall during the handstand. An extremely advanced version of this exercise is to alter it such that the supported somersault to handstand is going backward. I hesitate even to add it here because it requires a very advanced understanding of space and dynamics, with regard to moving backwards, and an acute ability to know where the wall is for the blind approach. This is not just advanced, but *very* advanced so be careful who you allow to do it. Any time you turn backwards with your head close to the wall there is the potential for injury.

 VIDEO REFERENCE 5.17. *Supported Forward Somersault with Handstand*

Vertical Run

From the L position, lower down into plank. Turn entire body to face the right. Shift harness so that the carabiner is at your left hip. Your body should create a "T" with the wall. Grab onto the rope with your left arm. Keep arm straight and raised up to head level, forming a triangle with the rope. Shoulders, pelvis and legs should be aligned horizontally. Place the feet in parallel second position. Run forward. When you reach the peak of the arc, pull the rope to the other side while switching your pelvis and harness so that the carabiner is on your right hip. Run forward. Repeat 8×.

Intermediate: Repeat exercise except do not hold on to the rope. Allow your arms to move as they would when you run. Use the strength of your pelvis and back to switch harness at the top of each arc.

Advanced: Repeat entire phrase with arms switching from first to second to fifth positions with each run.

 VIDEO REFERENCE 5.18. *Vertical Run*

Vertical Run with Superman

From the L position, lower down into plank. Turn entire body to face the right. Shift harness so that the carabiner is at your left hip. Your body should create a "T" with the wall. Grab on to the rope with your left arm. Keep arm straight and raised up to head level, forming a triangle with the rope. Shoulders, pelvis and legs should be aligned horizontally. Place the feet in parallel second position. Run forward. When you reach the peak of the arc, push off the wall with both legs. As you swing to the other side you will float through the air and your feet find the wall again at the height of the arc on the other side. Be sure that your abdominals are engaged, your back is long and the head, shoulder, pelvis, feet alignment is correct. The sequence I generally use is, run for 3 counts, push off on count 4, swing back 5, 6 land 7–8. Repeat 4×. Shift back to plank, making sure that the center part of your harness is at your belly button. Come up to L position. Rest. Repeat entire exercise on the left side.

Intermediate: Repeat entire exercise, except do not hold on to the rope. Bring your arms to a natural running position. On the push off, arms raise to fifth position and bring them back down upon the landing. Be aware that, due to their weight, your head and shoulders will probably want to drop down towards the ground, out of alignment. Pull your abdominals and your external obliques in tight and use the power in your arms to keep them strong and aligned. Repeat 4× to right. Shift back to plank, making sure that the center part of your harness is at your belly button. Come up to L position. Rest. Repeat entire exercise on the left. Work up to 8× per side.

Advanced: Repeat entire exercise with arms in second as you run and fifth position as you fly backwards. Repeat 4× to right. Shift back to plank, making sure that the center part of your harness is at your belly button. Come up to L position. Rest. Repeat entire exercise on the left. Work up to 8× per side.

 VIDEO REFERENCE 5.19. *Vertical Run with Superman*

Vertical Run with Somersault

From the L position, lower down into plank. Turn entire body to face the right. Shift harness so that the carabiner is at your left hip. Your body should create a "T" with the wall. Place the feet in parallel second position. Run forward. When you reach the peak of the arc, push off the wall with both legs and tuck your head and knees into a ball, turning toward the wall. Be sure that you use enough push-force and spinning-force to allow you to somersault before you reach the peak of the arc on the other side. Also be aware that your body needs to push away from the wall enough to fit your head and knees without scraping the surface. As you swing to the other side you will float through the air and your feet find the wall again at the height of the arc on the other side. The sequence I generally use is, run for 3 counts, push off on count 4, swing back 5, 6 land 7–8. Repeat 4×. Shift back to plank, making sure that the center part of your harness is at your belly button. Come up to L position. Rest. Repeat entire exercise to the left.

Intermediate: Repeat entire exercise, except do not hold on to the rope. Allow your arms to be in a typical running position. Be aware that, due to its weight, your head and shoulders will want to drop down towards the ground. You need to work to get your somersault parallel to the ground so that your shoulder, hip and knees are in alignment with one another. Pull your abdominals and your external obliques in tight and use your arms to hold tight to your knees. Repeat to right. Shift back to plank, making sure that the center part of your harness is at your belly button. Come up to L position. Rest. Repeat entire exercise to the left. Work up to 8× per side.

Advanced: Repeat entire exercise with arms in fifth position, pulling arms in during the somersault and extending again upon landing. Repeat 4× to right. Shift back to plank, making sure that the center part of your harness is at your belly button. Come up to L position. Rest. Repeat entire exercise to the left. Work up to 8× per side.

 VIDEO REFERENCE 5.20. *Vertical Run with Somersault*

Vertical Run with Forward Somersault to Handstand

Using the vertical run with somersault exercise as a base, here we add a handstand, which adds complexity because the run and somersault must be powerful but the handstand, in order to balance, must be gentle. Deftness in the use of force as well as how it is dispersed across the movement phrase is important here. From the L position, lower down into plank. Turn entire body to face the right. Shift harness so that the carabiner is at your left hip. Your body should create a "T" with the wall. Arms are released into first position. Run forward. When you reach the peak of the arc, push off the wall with both legs and tuck your head and knees into your chest, turning toward the wall with shoulders, hips and head in alignment and parallel to the ground. Be sure that you use enough push force and spinning force to allow you to somersault before you reach the peak of the arc on the other side. Also be aware that your body needs to push away from the wall enough to fit your head and knees without scraping the surface. As you swing to the other side, fully rotate the body, turning one and a half times, landing on your hands with elbows in plié and extending your head and torso out straight to side plank again. Watch your balance. At the end of the handstand, bring your feet back to the wall by bending at the waist and bringing them forward (the opposite direction of the way you just somersaulted). Repeat 4×. Shift back to plank, making sure that the center part of your harness is at your belly button. Come up to L position. Rest. Repeat exercise again on the same side 4× but, at the end of the handstand, flip onto your feet by continuing the motion of the spin with body outstretched in the handstand position. (Keep going in the same direction as the somersault.) Shift back to plank, making sure that the center part of your harness is at your belly button. Come up to L position. Rest. Repeat entire exercise on the other side.

Intermediate: Vary the tempo of the spins. Shorten time spent rebalancing and reorienting before and after flip and lengthen time in horizontal handstand plank position. Repeat with arms in fifth during runs.

Advanced: Try the phrase in the same way again except this time alter the vertical run so that you run backwards but then somersault forward to handstand. It may take one or two passes to get the momentum and the pendulum arc built up prior to executing the combination. Running backwards is a complex motion (even when you aren't on a vertical surface).

 VIDEO REFERENCE 5.21. *Vertical Run with Forward Somersault to Handstand*

Vertical Run Forward with Back Walkover

From the L position, lower down into plank. Turn entire body to face the right. Shift harness so that the carabiner is at your left hip. Your body should create a "T" with the wall. Arms are in first position. Run forward. When you reach the peak of the arc, push off the wall with your top leg (left) after passing through fifth position parallel follow with second leg close behind, extend your torso so it's long. Open your body, turning away from the wall with shoulders, hips, and head in alignment and parallel to the ground. As your hands come around, plié your elbows and push them off the wall (if you have enough force, your hands may not touch so you may want to extend your arms simply to protect your head from the wall). You will complete one back walkover. Be sure that you use enough push-force and spinning-force (torque) to allow you to complete the back walkover before you reach the peak of the arc on the other side. Also be aware that your body needs to push away from the wall enough to fit your head and extended upper torso without scraping the surface. Watch your balance. The sequence I generally use is: run forward for 4 counts, back walkover for 4 counts. You should end the walkover at the height of the swing arc on the opposite side. Repeat 4×. Shift back to plank, making sure that the center part of your harness is at your belly button. Come up to L position. Rest. Repeat entire exercise to the left side, making sure the top foot (right) passes through parallel fifth and leads as you begin the walkover.

Intermediate: Vary the tempo of the spins. Shorten time spent rebalancing and reorienting before and after flip.

Advanced: Vary the tempo of the spins. Shorten time spent rebalancing and reorienting before and after flip. Shift R to L after each walkover by adding one swing to the combination. Repeat 8×.

 VIDEO REFERENCE 5.22. *Vertical Run Forward with Back Walkover*

Vertical Run Backward with Front Walkover

From the L position, lower down into plank. Turn entire body to face the right. Shift harness so that the carabiner is at your left hip. Your body should create a "T" with the wall. Arms are released into first position. Run forward and backward a couple of times to create the pendulum arc you will need. This exercise begins backward. Run backward, when you reach the peak of the arc, push off the wall with your top leg (left) and follow with second leg close behind, extend your torso so it's long. Open your body, reaching forward with your arms. Be sure your hips and head are in alignment and parallel to the ground. As your hands come around, plié your elbows and push them off the wall (if you have enough force, your hands may not touch so simply extend your arms to protect your head from the wall.) You will complete one forward walkover. Be sure that you use enough push-force and spinning-force (torque) to allow you to complete the front walkover before you reach the peak of the arc on the other side. Also be aware that your body needs to push away from the wall enough to fit your head and extended upper torso without scraping the surface and carry you around to your feet. (Many students land on their rear ends so be sure to get your feet under you.) Watch your balance. The sequence I generally use is: run backward for 4 counts, front walkover for 4 counts. You should end the walkover at the height of the swing arc on the opposite side. Repeat 4×. Shift back to plank, making sure that the center part of your harness is at your belly button. Come up to L position. Rest. Repeat entire exercise to the left side, making sure the right foot leads as you begin the flip, pushing off with left foot.

Intermediate: Vary the tempo of the spins. Shorten time spent rebalancing and reorienting before and after flip.

Advanced: Vary the tempo of the spins. Shorten time spent rebalancing and reorienting before and after flip. Shift R to L after each walkover by adding one swing to the combination. Repeat 8×.

 VIDEO REFERENCE 5.23. *Vertical Run Backward with Front Walkover*

NOTE

Any exercises that include vertical running or swinging will naturally include residual swing. I haven't addressed that in each exercise but will do so in a general way here. First, it's unavoidable. For most of these exercises (and certainly when you choreograph and perform) this type of momentum is desired and, even necessary, for continuity. When we are performing isolated exercises that aren't combined into phrases, the best way to put on the brakes is to shift your pelvis back to center. Make sure the carabiner and grigri is centered on your torso at your belly button. At the same time, extend the leg that is closest to the direction you are swinging as far out to the side as possible. Push against the swing. Do the same thing to the other side. This will help to center your body after side-to-side exercises. When teaching class, you can include 2–4 extra swings at the end of the exercise so that the class ends together in an organized fashion. When moving onto the phrase portion of the class, it is helpful to organize the phrases such that specific movements are included between swinging steps that will enable the dancers to center themselves and/or include swinging or running into phrases that will naturally calm the pendulum. For example, I've found that if you've just finished vertical running with front walkovers and have a ton of side-to-side momentum built up, you could follow that up with a movement that makes use of the residual swing but also calms it. Flip splits are a good example because the energy in that exercise is outward (away from the wall) and because the motion of the movement involves powerful leg motions that are perpendicular to the direction of the swing, it will help to quiet the swing in a natural way. (It also has the added benefit of looking pretty cool.) You can follow up this movement with something more stationary, or controlled.

CHAPTER 6

Phrases

Traveling Through Space

This is the portion of class that has always been my favorite as a dancer. Putting together the individual steps into phrases while incorporating musicality, form, time, and quality. *Dancing.* It feels as if this is the culmination of all the hard work. In traditional forms, a dancer may feel total abandon in a wide, open studio with, seemingly, limitless time and space. There is nothing so freeing as filling up that space with movement. Aerial presents the dancer with a new sort of freedom. One that opens up new avenues but also presents challenges to the deeply held

Figure 6.01 Freedom in flight
Credit: © Washington and Lee University 2009

dance canon. It's peculiar, in some ways, to compare aerial dance with freedom because there are many ways in which the aerial dancer is compromised. She has (in my case) a 2.5 pound harness attached to her body, is tied to a rope which limits circular motion and other movements typical in traditional dance. The dancer is supporting hardware and helmet while she moves and gravitational forces interact with the body and alignment in new and unusual ways. For these reasons, aerial technique is a movement form that reflects traditional dance but can't quite mimic it. As a response, we generate a new system of conditioning specific to the stresses we've inadvertently placed on the human body. In my opinion, aerial isn't necessarily about freedom of movement but about being able to move in ways not possible in traditional dance. One must give up things in order to achieve this goal. For example, in the case of my rigging system, the dancer's face is never fully exposed to the audience unless she is upside down, and only partially, if she's sideways or spinning. Certainly that can be looked upon as a freedom from traditional theatrics or typical expectations, but I'd be lying if I didn't say it was sometimes frustrating. True freedom in dance would allow flight with no limitations, but unless and until we start choreographing in zero gravity (which would present its own challenges), or sprout wings (also challenging!), aerial remains imperfect. Honestly, for me, that's exactly what makes aerial exciting. I view the challenges as opportunities to discover new and usual ways of moving through space.

Below are some combinations that I use in class. Any of these exercises can be manipulated and shuffled to create new combinations with new shapes and ideas. I include these because I feel like they are a good mix of inverting, turning, and spinning at various speeds and they take into consideration forces pressing or pulling the aerialist. I think that they constitute a good basis for work in balance and coordination as well as concepts in force, energy, and space. One thing I find interesting about phrase work (and all aerial really) is that everything can change with a small adjustment of a few feet of rope higher or lower. The body has to completely reorient itself if the movement is just a little faster or a few beats slower. Combine these, seemingly small variables, and everything changes. For this reason, among many, it's so very important that a student's proprioceptors are challenged daily by switching up timing within phrases and height on the wall. It's important for our bodies to learn what they can do at any given height with any tempo of music and know how hard to push, how fast to spin, how slow to react, how to control the time and body motion as we move through space. Through repetition and rehearsal we learn how to deal with these irrevocable forces and handle them with grace, with power, with specific timing, and, with what appears to be, ease. An aerialist is dancing with a mind that is working ten times as fast as the body, feeling what can't be seen and anticipating what might or might not happen.

I do not consider these phrases choreography, as they aren't organized in any way other than to work the previous exercises within a larger context and with specific goals. Put another way, we are putting the words (individual exercises) we learned previously into sentences (phrases). In this way the students' agility, coordination and ability to solve new, emerging problems is tested. Connecting movements is a challenge because it combines strength and endurance with agility, balance and precision; elements that appear to be at odds. It is necessary to use the correct muscle groups and work with force and energy to accomplish a task and

Figure 6.02 Challenges in flight

do it with proper alignment and specificity. Below are a few standards that I use. Each phrase challenges the aerialist in a different way, but focuses on basic skill sets typically used in choreographic works. Any of the previous exercises can be combined in myriads of ways to create phrases like the ones below, so feel free to mix and match.

Phrase #1

(Goals: shifting from L to plank, shifting from plank to T position)

Beginning in the L position, swing RLRL.

Swing R, arabesque turn.

Swing RL arabesque turn.

As soon as arabesque lands at height of the arc on the R, flatten out to plank while cartwheeling to the L. Stay in plank. Cartwheel to R.

Turn pelvis to face the L, carabiner at R hip, grab on to rope with R hand to complete assisted back walkover. Repeat.

Shift body to plank (carabiner is at belly button), plié and push away from the wall into starfish. Repeat 2×. Finish in plank. Come up to L position. Rest.

Repeat entire phrase to the other side.

 VIDEO REFERENCE 6.1. *Phrase 1*

Phrase #2

(Goals: Maintaining correct alignment in side plank position. Shifting positions while moving through space)

Beginning in L position, shift pelvis to the R (carabiner on L hip).

Run 3 steps, hop up with arms in fifth position while swinging back. Repeat.

Run 3 steps, at very top of arc, flip pelvis to other side.

Swing L with legs in leap position and body facing the swing.

Open double arabesque turn.

Cartwheel L.

Swing to the right.

At top of arc, flip carabiner to right hip. As you swing back to L, somersault 2×.

Swing RLR in L position gradually shrinking pendulum swing to stillness.

Repeat entire phrase on other side.

 VIDEO REFERENCE 6.2. *Phrase 2*

Phrase #3

(Goals: Controlling power when pushing away. Implementing smooth transitions between motion and stationary work)

Beginning in plank position, push away to starfish. Land.

Arabesque turn to R.

Repeat push away starfish and arabesque turn to L.

Walk up wall, lower body down to inverted spin.

Spin 4 counts without stopping.

End spin facing away from the wall. Release legs from rope. Walk legs down the wall moving
   body into plank. Hold.

Plié and push away, half turn to plank with arms against the wall. Hold. Repeat plié and half
   turn to plank with arms – finishing the circle feet on the wall.

Turn pelvis to R (carabiner at L hip) forward walkover, back walkover. Repeat.

Turn to plank.

Repeat entire phrase on other side.

 VIDEO REFERENCE 6.3. *Phrase 3*

Phrase #4

(Goals: Inverting while stationary and while moving. Achieving fluid transitions between inverting and reverting)

From L position lower down to plank.

Torso flip lifting R leg. Plié and push, arms reach down to the floor.

Finish torso flip continuing in same direction, lifting L leg. Plié and push, arms reach out.

Starfish with legs closed, R cartwheel. Repeat 2×.

Swing RLRL.

Split flip jump (as you swing side to side) RL.

Flip pelvis to R (carabiner at L hip), vertical run with hop.

Flip pelvis to L (carabiner at R hip) backward walkover.

Repeat vertical run with hop and backward walkover.

Swing RLRL lowering pendulum back to stationary L.

Repeat entire phrase on other side.

 VIDEO REFERENCE 6.4. *Phrase 4*

Phrase #5

(Goals: Changing pelvis positions while in transition. Changing direction of swing quickly)

From L position, lower to plank.

Flip torso to R (carabiner on L hip).

Ball spin, land, push away from wall, legs together, arms reaching out (superman), Repeat.

Back walkover.

Swing RLR, arabesque turn 2×.

Swing LR, ball turn 2×.

Pencil turn 2×.

2 starfish.

Repeat entire exercise on other side.

 VIDEO REFERENCE 6.5. *Phrase 5*

Phrase #6

(Goals: Implementing fine motor skills, balance, agility)

From L position, jog RLRL.

Drop to back bend and come to plank.

R leg torso flip.

Push away from wall as you come back to plank (push legs against wall, body flies away
     from wall and leg unwinds from rope and both legs return to wall, body in plank).

Cartwheel to R.

Small push off into ball spin to R.

Split L leg front.

Half turn into handstand (head to wall) R.

Walk arms down wall and wrap legs around rope (chest is against wall).

Spin one and a half times.

Walk feet down wall to return to L position.

Repeat entire exercise on the other side.

 VIDEO REFERENCE 6.6. *Phrase 6*

Phrase #7

(Goals: Cultivate coordination, practice timing and balance)

Swing RLR, closed leg arabesque turn. Repeat turn to the R.

Chassé (step, together, step) into cartwheel to R.

Back walkover as swing back to L.

Run 3 steps to the R supported back walkover.

Run 3 steps to the R supported back flip.

Push off (keeping pelvis to side) superman 2×.

Land, somersault front, somersault back.

Plank into L.

Repeat entire exercise on the other side.

 VIDEO REFERENCE 6.7. *Phrase 7*

Phrase #8

(Goals: Building strength, successful changes of direction in the air, developing endurance)

L position to plank.

Shift to R side (carabiner at L hip).

Turning side handstand, hold, plié elbows.

Arch back and roll through back bend to stand in T on wall.

Front walkover, back walkover. Repeat 2×.

Torso flip R, plié.

Push legs against wall, body flies away from wall and leg unwinds from rope and both legs
    return to wall, body in plank.

Back bend.

Turn to wall.

Plank, plié elbows, push away.

Half turn to plank.

Starfish 2×.

Repeat entire exercise to the other side.

 VIDEO REFERENCE 6.8. *Phrase 8*

CHAPTER 7

Cool Down

Cooling down is integral to the success of the dancer. At this point in the class, the students are exhausted. Their muscles are tired, they are *very* sweaty and, frequently, their bodies are hurting from the abrasions of the harness and hardware. As soon as they descend from the

Figure 7.01 Stretching is a necessary component of the cool down
Credit: © Washington and Lee University 2009

wall, we begin a stretching series. This is partially because, due to the gravitational angle in relationship to our bodies, there is little opportunity to stretch while rigged. Additionally, post-workout is the perfect time to work on lengthening the muscles while they are warm and elastic.

Before we completely disengage from the equipment, I ask the students to lower themselves down so that they can stand on the floor. (This immediately relieves some of the aches of the harness in the upper and inner thigh region.) We unclip from the front of the harness and clip in to the point at the center of the waist in the back. BE SURE not to clip into the equipment loops. Not all harnesses have a back loop so, if you do this exercise, be sure you are wearing one that does.

WALL STRETCH

Tabletops

Standing on the floor, clipped in from the lower back, gently drop your torso down to your feet and hold. Feel the hamstrings. Drop the head, keeping the legs straight and stretch. Hold. Plié both legs and slowly slide them out to the back. You should be hanging from the center back point and your body should close up like an inverted V. Hang. Arms and legs are bent. Balance on the clip-in point. Slowly raise the arms and legs up, forming a straight line with your body. Arms and feet reach out long, face is towards the floor but head is in line with the arms. Hold for 8. Lower down for 8. Repeat 4×.

 VIDEO REFERENCE 7.1. *Tabletop*

Handstand

In this exercise we use the rope and harness just as a safety feature without really engaging it. Stay clipped in to the back of your harness. Face the wall, take a step forward and kick both legs up, one at a time, raising them to the wall. Be sure to engage your abdominals, keeping arms straight and shoulders and head aligned. Push out of your shoulders. Hold. Come down and repeat. For those with tired arms, this can also be done on elbows. Just be sure your rope is long enough for you to get down that low. Since you don't get a ton of opportunity to work your arms in aerial, if your class has enough energy and strength, the extended arm position is a great opportunity for a few push ups.

 VIDEO REFERENCE 7.2. *Handstand*

Splits

For this, you must unharness yourself from the rope completely. Just unclip the carabiner and grigri and keep the harness on. Place the ascender back on the rope at about face height. Grab onto the ascender with one or both hands, lower down into a split. If you can't get all the way down, use your arms to balance yourself with the ascender. Hold. Repeat on other side. Repeat in center.

 VIDEO REFERENCE 7.3. *Splits*

FLOOR STRETCH

At this point, generally, the students collapse on the floor. Luckily, this stretching and cool down series takes place on the floor, so happiness abounds. Below is an example of what I share verbally during floor stretching and cooling down. This isn't always the same every class. I base some of the floor stretch and cool down on the solicited and unsolicited feed-back I received during class. ("This is killing my inner thighs/left shoulder/abdominals.") While usually quite hyperbolic, classwork feedback gives me a feel for what the students need. ("What did I do to deserve this?" and "Why do you hate me?" are a bit more difficult to associate with stretches.) I also use feedback mentioned in previous classes during the "ice pack response" period. (This is mentioned on p. 96 under Closing Class.) At this point the students can remove their harnesses and place them off to the side. I recommend they open the harnesses as much as possible so that they can dry during the remainder of the class.

Hamstrings, Back, Arms, and Pelvis

Lay flat on the ground in constructive rest. Your back is released down into the floor. Knees are bent up to the ceiling and feet are flat on the floor. Feet are aligned with the ischial tuberosities. Arms are out to the sides with palms up. Be sure that your palms are a little bit lower than your shoulders so that your scapulae are in place. Close your eyes. Release all the tension, stress, and tightness. Let it flow into the floor. Bring the right leg into the chest, reach around below the knee with both hands to stretch. Hold. Cross the foot that's in the air (R) over the thigh of the other leg, allow that entire shape to fall to the left side. The right side of your pelvis will come off the floor and both knees/legs will be over to the left. In this position, press both shoulders down, with focus on the right shoulder. Press both knees to the floor. You will feel a long stretch across the body. Slide the right arm along the floor towards your head. At the head, lift the elbow up so it comes up and over your head, keep sliding it over to the other arm. Place it on top of the other arm. Feel your shoulders line up. The underneath arm reaches down to grab the knee that's on top (right). Pull the knee up to your chest while keeping it on the floor. Roll your pelvis over so it's flat on the floor. The right side of your ribs (which are in the air) will roll forward onto the floor. Lengthen your left leg so it's straight and flat on the floor. Keep holding onto that knee and you will feel a stretch across the back of the arm that's underneath you.. Keep pulling the knee up towards your chest and feel the stretch behind the leg and across the front of the pelvis. Hold. Open up the front of your pelvis and let it sink down into the floor. Press down the left side. Lengthen long out of the straightened left leg. Feel it press away from your pelvis. Straighten the bent leg (your right leg), grab the ankle with both hands and pull it close to your chest while keeping it on the floor. Keep pressing your pelvis down to the floor. Hold. Grab the foot with both hands and roll onto your back, initiating the movement from the center of your back. Stretch leg up to the ceiling, holding onto it with both hands. Other leg rolls back and is straight out from the body. Release your head and shoulders down. Soften in the pelvis. Release behind the outstretched knee and release the leg down to the floor, placing the foot flat. Allow the other leg to come up to meet it so it's flat on the floor. You are back in constructive rest. Repeat entire exercise to the other side.

 VIDEO REFERENCE 7.4. *Hamstrings, Back, Arms, and Pelvis*

Lumbar, Psoas, and Hamstrings

Pull both knees into the chest, roll body over to the right side and then onto your knees. You will be in child's pose. Extend arms long. Allow the body to fold. Breathe deeply through your back. Allow your back to feel wide. Hold. Slowly raise torso so you are sitting on your ankles. Hands pressing to either side, lift your weight off your body and press one leg (right) back long and straight and allow the other leg to rise to the foot with a bent knee. Making sure the bent knee is directly over the ankle, press long through the extended leg, reaching the back heel away from the body. At the same time press down into the acetabulum and forward toward your front heel, holding your weight in your hands that are on either side of the bent knee. Hold. Reach your head up; arch your upper back while dropping your pelvis down. Hold. Lift your pelvis up to the ceiling, bring both legs straight (feet in fourth position parallel). Reach your head long to the floor and in to the front leg. Hold. Bring legs together, straight and hang. Plié on both legs. Lift your heels and use your hands to lower your body back to the floor. Drop knees, untuck toes, lower torso and come back to child's pose. Repeat the entire exercise on the other side.

 VIDEO REFERENCE 7.5. *Lumbar, Psoas, and Hamstrings*

Psoas, Pelvis, and Torso

Walk your hands back to your torso to help you sit up on your knees. Sit your pelvis to the right side of your feet. Swing legs out from under your body to the side and then the front.

Bend knees, turning them out and bringing them into the body. Tuck one leg close to your pelvis with knee out to the side. Bring second leg in the same position directly on top of the first leg. Line up your knees vertically one on top of the other. Sit tall on your ischial tuberosities, back long and head reaching to the ceiling. Hold. Gently lower your torso over your knees, softening and opening in the acetabulum. Hold. Repeat with legs in reversed positions.

 VIDEO REFERENCE 7.6. *Psoas, Pelvis, and Torso*

Chest, Neck, and Sides

Place both hands on floor in front of knees. Release top leg to the side and unfold body to the right, rolling onto your stomach. Release down into the floor. Feel your rib cage widen and open. Elongate across your shoulder girdle. Hands on either side of your chest, gently push with your hands so that your head and chest raise off the floor. Arch in your back gently, and reach your head long to the wall behind you to stretch your abdominals. Hold. Repeat. Lower back down so you are flat on your front. Slide your torso and your legs to the right, forming a C shape with your body. Do not allow your pelvis or shoulders to come off the floor. Release your obliques and transverse abdominis. Hold. Repeat to the other side. Repeat entire exercise.

 VIDEO REFERENCE 7.7. *Chest, Neck, and Sides*

Constructive Rest

Roll back onto your back. Come back to constructive rest. Close your eyes and sink down into the floor. Using an ideokinetic approach, take a mental inventory of your body. In your mind's eye, begin at the top of your head and work slowly down through the body to your feet, noting places of soreness or tiredness, areas of strength, places of special interest due to previous injury, build up of lactic acid or other factors. Note areas that have changed or gotten stronger due to previous classes. What areas feel tired but strong? In what area should you take extra caution for the next class? Is there something you should pay attention to in future? Make mental notes. Slowly open your eyes and come back to the present.

 VIDEO REFERENCE 7.8 *Constructive Rest*

CLOSING CLASS

I usually keep a bunch of ice packs in a nearby freezer. At this point, students who feel they need it, grab one or two. Be sure that the students' bodies have cooled down significantly before applying ice. You don't want to shock their systems by applying freezing cold compresses to warm muscles. These ice bags are for sore spots due to abrasions from the harness. Usually students sit on the floor with their legs outstretched in front of them with an ice pack in between their upper thighs. This is the area that gets most irritated by the harness. They ice for about 15 minutes and I use that time to elicit feedback, participate in discussion and give clarifications. I tend to ask questions like "What was harder (or easier) then expected?" "Where do you feel you were successful?" "In what areas do you feel you need to work?" "What was fun and what was simply arduous?" I use this time for assessment so I can learn how they are feeling about the material and their understanding of themselves. Many times, if they make salient points, I adjust the sequence or intensity of various things based on their feedback. Because it's virtually impossible to demonstrate, give directions, correct, and watch all of the students at the same time, this feedback is vital for the development of the class. Keep in mind that the height and weight of the dancers as well as their conditioning can affect the difficulty of some movements and therefore everyone may not be sore in the same places or give similar feedback in terms of pain management. Although the students' responses may vary widely in terms of which phrases or exercises are difficult or easy, many times this is attributable to their natural physical gifts or challenges. The important thing here is to ask, *Why?* Why something is difficult or easy for a student may give you insight into the strengths or weaknesses of the individual student and/or gives you clues as to whether they are correctly executing the movement. It may also help you to create variations for those in need. For example, one of my students had a terrible time with the torso flip. He indicated that his leg kept hitting his carabiner and he couldn't get it over to the other side. I watched him closely in class and determined that not only were his hamstrings very tight but he had limited mobility in his pelvis, both of which are necessary for the torso flip. Once I ascertained the issue and figured out the *why*, I gave him a work around. I explained that he could plié on his standing leg which helped with the pelvic mobility and adapted the leg so it swung over in attitude, which caused him not to have to overstrain his hamstrings. Once the accommodations were made, he was able to do the movement. After getting the feedback, I added hamstring stretches into the beginning of the cool down sequence while their bodies are still very warm. This is an example of assimilating individual student feedback as a means of developing the class syllabus more fully so that variations to the exercises can be incorporated into the regular class.

Post-Class

EQUIPMENT CLEAN UP

It's important to create a clean up system for the end of class that happens in the same way every time. I generally assign specific duties to each student that they are responsible for. This has the dual benefit of giving the students a sense of ownership in the class and knowing who to find if someone doesn't do their job properly (!)

Utility Bags

Since there are many pieces to an aerial rig, we purchased individual bags for each student. The bags we bought are a breathable material that has small holes throughout so that moisture is wicked away and the temperature within the bag remains stable. At the top of the bag is a drawstring with a clasp so it can be closed. One facet of the bag that I love is that it has a flat bottom. The bottom enables the bags to be lined up in rows in the storage box. This discourages the students from laying them on top of one another, which defeats the goal of keeping them moisture free and at a constant temperature. Inside the bag we placed one carabiner, one grigri and one ascender with attached leg loop. Each bag was given a number matching the one each student was assigned. This way, the student is responsible for his/her own equipment and gets to know its idiosyncrasies. This also makes it easier to locate changes in the equipment from one class to the next when doing safety checks. At the end of class, the student collects their equipment and replaces it properly within the bag. (If any piece of equipment gets dropped or broken during the class, it is permanently retired and a new piece of equipment takes its place.) At the end of the semester the carabiners', grigris' and ascenders' joints (gates and hinges) should be blown out with compressed air, to get rid of small particles that might be hampering the locking mechanisms, and lubricant should be added if needed. The equipment can be washed in warm, mild soapy water, if needed, but since we primarily work inside we've never had to do this. If washed, they have to be dried thoroughly. The leg loop can be spot cleaned with mild soap and/or water and then laid out to dry (not in the sun).

Figure 8.01 Equipment must be treated with care
Credit: © Washington and Lee University 2009

Harnesses

The harnesses are taken off and, during the floor cool down and response period, laid out in the classroom – not in sunlight – to dry. (They are usually wet from sweat.) At the end of class, each harness is placed in its own bag, which allows for further drying due to venting in the bag and also ensures that the harness doesn't get pulls or tears in it during storage. Since we work indoors, we've never had to clean our harnesses. But, in the event that you need to, spot cleaning with water is best. If necessary, you can spot clean with mild soap and water but you shouldn't submerge the harnesses in water. Use a cloth or soft tooth brush on stubborn areas. They should be dried away from direct sunlight.

Helmets

At the end of class, helmets are taken off and towel dried. They are left in the cabinet upside down with the attachment points lying out to the sides of the helmet. Ensuring that the chinstraps aren't bent or crumpled encourages fast drying. Years ago, prior to coming to the university, my students had to share helmets. After a few classes, we noticed that they were getting rashes on their foreheads where the suspension framework inside the helmet comes in contact with their skin. I kept a container of Lysol wipes with the aerial equipment and the students used them to wipe the interior structure of the helmet to get rid of any bacteria. The rashes went away but I soon learned (luckily, not the hard way) that this is a very bad cleaning process. Any type of harsh detergent or cleaning chemical can weaken the helmet. Each of my students has their own helmet and we simply wash them with room temperature soap (hand soap not bacterial) and water at the end of the semester. Since we don't use the helmets in the outdoors, the shell doesn't get dirty but, if it should, the same soap and water cleaning process is fine.

Cabinet

One of my colleagues at my university graciously built me a custom made cabinet for the aerial equipment. If it's possible to do this, I highly recommend it as it can be designed to suit your specific needs. My cabinet is about 5 feet tall and 3 feet wide. It's on wheels so I can move it wherever I need it and it has a locking mechanism on the outside of the door for safety. The top third of the cabinet contains 6 drawers where I can store clipboards and safety check sheets, extra carabiners and grigris and any other small equipment that I may need. I always store the students' completed safety tests there as well. The middle portion of the cabinet is divided into two large boxes. The bags that contain all the equipment are stored on one side and the helmets are stored on the other. The bottom third of the cabinet is one big space where the bagged harnesses are kept. This type of organization is very nice both for the recording and safe keeping of all of your equipment and it aids in teaching the students how and where things are stored so equipment is not lost. If you don't have access to custom cabinetry, think deeply about your needs and find something that will help you store everything properly.

Ropes

The ropes I use in class are rigged to a catwalk so, following class, the students walk up to the catwalk to put away the ropes. We have one large bucket that sits between every two ropes. Once the equipment is removed from the rope, the students pull up the ropes to the catwalk, gently coil the rope (be careful not to bend the rope too sharply and definitely do not wrap it around your elbow and hand to coil it as that weakens the supportive structure inside) and place the rope in the buckets. In this way, the rope stays off the catwalk so it isn't stepped on or tripped over, it's safe from snags and tears and it's ready to be let down for the next class.

SAFETY IN CLEAN UP

Equipment Safety

All of the equipment for aerial must be kept away from chemicals, extremes of heat or cold, sunlight and any sort of objects that can abrade, rip, dent or crack them. Where your storage box is stored and where the ropes are rigged, must be kept in a climate controlled environment. Any large fluctuations in temperature one way or the other can damage the equipment. Extremes of heat are especially bad. It's a good idea for each piece of equipment to be stored in a soft bag before being put into the storage box. (This is especially true for harnesses if your box is made of unsanded wood.) Large buckets are great for the ropes as there is nothing to snag or tear the rope. As with any safety information in this book, *please refer to the equipment's recommended washing and maintaining directions.* Every piece of equipment is different and even different manufacturers of the same equipment may have different rules for maintaining and cleaning. All of the information above and within the book are simply my experiences. I am not a certified rigger so check with your official supplier for particulars. Doing this is not only a safety issue but, if done properly, it can lengthen the life of your equipment.

People Safety

If you are lucky enough to be working with colleagues who understand or specialize in aerial work, it's a good idea to have a third set of eyes on everything you do. The wonderful technical director at my university inspects all of the equipment, both the individual pieces in the storage box and the rig itself, on a weekly basis. In this way, the students do a daily check for themselves and on each other as they are putting the equipment on and filling out their safety checklist in pairs, I move around the room and recheck as the students are filling out their safety forms, the students interact with the equipment again at the end of class, and a third person is checking weekly. The more eyes on everything, the more chance of success.

CHAPTER 9

Wellness

SIDE EFFECTS

Pay close attention to the health of your students. Some students may be feeling nauseous from the spinning and swinging and others may have headaches from being upside down. A few, who are deathly afraid of heights, may experience symptoms of anxiety. These are all common conditions in aerial. I've found that, with most students, these complaints lessen and go away over time. The students just need to be patient. The body needs a chance to adapt. The length of time it takes for the student to adjust to aerial is individual. Generally, when I teach an intensive class, every day for 5–6 hours per day, it takes about a week for the dancers to feel good doing it. When I teach a standard, semester long class, it takes longer because we aren't meeting as frequently or for as long a time in each class. Because of the intense nature of the form and the fact that everyone reacts differently, it's important for students to determine for themselves if they are up to it. I feel that it's the instructor's job to teach the students how to listen to their bodies and to help them learn to discern the difference between natural by-products of the classwork and something more sinister. I don't feel it's safe for me to judge what's best for them but I can guide them in discovering it for themselves. In general, I give the students a week or two to deal with pain or illness and allow them to sit out when needed, but I do ask that they try again after resting. A good rule of thumb is that if they can't live within this structure, they probably won't last through the semester. In this case, it's best to drop out of the class.

REST

I've found over the years that students can participate for a longer period on the wall if they have frequent, but short, rest periods. For this reason, I split my class into two groups. I teach a series of exercises to the group on the wall then they come down and rest while I review the same series with the second group. I repeat this throughout the class period. Although it sounds as if, with this method, a class would take twice as long, it really doesn't. The group that is resting on the floor watches and learns with the group on the wall as I go through the sequences step-by-step. By the time it's the second group's turn on the wall, they've watched me teach it and watched the other group perform it, so they don't need further instruction.

Figure 9.01 Dizziness, headache and nausea are common complaints
Credit: © Washington and Lee University 2009

Sometimes complex switches in the air or momentum changes need to be reviewed with the second group but most often, not. Over the course of the semester, the teaching time between groups gets shorter as they absorb the basic vocabulary. The time between groups lengthens again as phrasing becomes longer and richer. At one point a few years ago, I was worried that the resting group's time was being wasted so I devised a set of stretches and strength building exercises that they could do on the floor while waiting for their turn on the wall. I learned fast that this was a bad idea for two reasons: 1) the students actually DID need to rest. Their time wasn't being wasted because they were recuperating, drinking, breathing and regaining enough strength to be able to work again and 2) It's virtually impossible for me to teach, what was basically, two different classes at the same time. There wasn't enough of me to go around and everyone got short changed. So, lesson learned. Resting is not time wasted. In fact, it gives the student the opportunity to participate more over the long term. This is also a kindness to their bodies. Because they are taking time to recuperate during class, they aren't hobbling home from class and unable to move the next day (usually).

WATER

I can't stress enough how important water is to the health of the aerial dancer (and to everyone, obviously). This class is intensely aerobic and anaerobic at the same time. It's easy to get lulled into the fun of aerial and forget that it's an incredibly intense experience. Every time a student gets a break from the wall, they need to drink. It's important not to overfill the stomach because it's likely that in 10 minutes or so they will have to spin upside down again. Consistent, small drinks are vital. I require the students to bring water bottles and, due to the nature of the class, they get short but frequent rest and water breaks. For some, water with electrolytes is a great help in dealing with fatigue in class. I had a student once who brought frozen grapes to class. This is a nice idea because grapes provide hydration and also a little sugar. Just be sure not to rely solely on fruit as it won't provide enough hydration on it's own.

FOOD

Having spoken about water, I feel it incumbent upon me to also briefly mention food. I won't go into what it means to be a healthy eater because there is a lot of literature on the subject written by people way more qualified than I. However, I would like to talk about timing. Aerial dance is intense. There is a lot of spinning and a lot of upside down-ness and your abdominals are taxed virtually all the time. Clearly, a full stomach is not a good partner for this sort of activity. One year, we were performing at the Corcoran Gallery of Art in Washington DC and two of my students were performing a duet on rope and harness that was a full 6 minutes of hanging upside down and spinning, intercut with long swings side to side. You can only imagine how taxing on the stomach that must have been. They never mentioned until after the performance that they didn't eat anything all day prior to rehearsal or performance for fear of what might happen. That's a real fear for aerialists, especially when performing, but I don't advocate this methodology. Eating something light that contains protein and drinking milk a few hours before class is a good idea. Give yourself something to help your bones and muscles and eat something that will fill you up but not be heavy. Allow yourself enough time to digest. (The digesting is important!) Then keep drinking water throughout. When I teach intensively, I usually plan a lunch break that lasts 2–3 hours. This way the students can eat something light that's easily digestible (and drink more!) and have time to digest before class begins again. I suggest eggs with black beans, almond butter toast, high protein oatmeal with bananas or kefir with fruit in the morning. It's light on your stomach but also packs a protein punch with carbohydrates and a little sugar. Cheese is good too. Don't drink tea or coffee as they are diuretics and will work against water retention. Tuna is a great lunch that's light but protein packed and veggies of any kind are great. Tomatoes, carrots and celery are light and provide vital nutrients or a simple salad with some crackers can be filling yet light. Give yourself time to rest before and after eating. If you've had class or rehearsal, allow your body to come to room temperature, drink water, then take time to eat lunch. It's always a good idea to wait an hour or more before resuming activities. (Since I'm writing now about taking long lunch breaks between aerial workouts, it reminds me of another important fact. It has nothing to do with eating, but nonetheless bears mentioning. When I have a long lunch break built into my class, I am always cognizant of re-warming up the body slowly. The tendency is to feel as if you've already done everything you need to do to warm up, but in three hours you can become cold and tight again. When returning to the wall, remember to take time. Even though you've already worked out, you aren't warm.)

Caring for Your Students

COMMUNICATING

There is much false information in the world about pushing yourself, working through exhaustion and embracing pain. I am very weary of any of this sort of talk. Dance, like any athletic endeavor, requires high-energy resources and challenges the dancer to strive to be better. This can range from physical to emotional to psychological challenges. While it's important to work hard and challenge oneself, every dancer would be well served to be aware of their limitations as well. I feel it incumbent upon the teacher to be very upfront with the demands of the form and have an honest discussion with any student who would like to participate. Aerial is taxing on the muscles, aerobically challenging, for those with fear of heights (and even for some without), frightening, and challenges even the most advanced dancer or athlete. Aerial is not for the fainthearted. It requires the performer to be very high off the ground. It requires inverting, spinning, and speed. It requires the aerialist to appear to be out of control while maintaining control. The aerialist needs strength to carry out movements correctly and there is the ever-present vertical surface, which the aerialist is only within a few inches of hitting at any given time. Additionally, the unusual forces endured by the dancer mean that it doesn't matter how much padding is built into the harness, they will finish rehearsal with black and blue marks, burns, scrapes and very sore muscles. Aerial dance takes a commitment. I think it's important to be very clear with your students about the challenges inherent in aerial dance before they begin. I've had students in the past who have signed up for my aerial class in order to "get over" something. Whether it's fear of heights or motion sickness, they feel that by forcing themselves to do what scares them, they will force themselves out of their fear. While I commend anyone who is brave enough to work through his or her fears, this motivation has seen little success in my classroom. More times than not, the student ends up dropping the class. Aerial is such an intense form that even students who have no anxiety and are completely physically fit are challenged. The technique is demanding in itself so adding any burden beyond the technique makes it almost impossible. Further, there really isn't an option to frequently sit out of class. If a student stops attending classes for weeks at a time because they are scared or feel ill, they

Figure 10.01 Awareness of your students' needs is crucial
Credit: © Washington and Lee University 2009

miss too much material and experiential learning and fall behind. (Of course, my experience is based on a twelve-week semester. I'd be interested to know if the class was taught over a full year at a slower pace, if the results would vary.) Having said this, there are always a few students that soldier on and gut it out. They have my utmost respect. They are battling numerous demons simultaneously. If such a situation occurs, I advise having a talk with any student who is using aerial for personal purposes. I speak with them about their goals, try to make them aware of what they are signing up for and determine, as best as I can, based on knowing them and their specific situation, whether I think they can be successful. I never try to talk them out of the class. I'm just honest with them. Once they make a decision, I fully support it. The worst case scenario is that if the student does end up dropping the class, they've still been exposed a little bit to something wonderful.

LISTENING

Because the effects of aerial dance are so individual, this means that functioning within the form happens on a case-by-case basis. Everyone has to decide for themselves what they can achieve and how far they can push themselves. I cannot and will not force anyone to participate on a given level. I think that for instructors of aerial (at least on the student level) effort must be made to assess each student based on where they started and how far they've come. This may mean expecting more from students who have no fear of heights or giving allowances to the student who has no athletic or dance experience. In the classroom, growth is important. Having said all of this though, one of the responsibilities of the aerialist is to open a dialogue within himself that becomes a pathway for body and mind communication. Self-assessment needs to be constant and an ongoing conversation should be happening within each dancer throughout the class. I explain to my students, for example, that if, during self assessment, one of them is reflecting on their strengths and weaknesses and he makes notes that his right ankle is weak and feels vulnerable, then my expectation is that, when he is on the wall, he chooses to leave out specific ankle rotation exercises or movements which return to the wall with force on his ankle. This self-selection process is vital in this form because injury can be detrimental to the entire process and could force the removal of a student for the entire semester. The difficulty with this, however, is that many students do not have a baseline from which to evaluate themselves. Additionally, there usually is someone whose judgment may be tinged with a competitive streak or, conversely, a student who tends to equate a simple lack of comfort with a potential for injury. It makes sense that new aerialists may not have the experience to know what it feels like to be close to an injury or the difference between exhaustion from a class and exhaustion partying the night before. In these cases self-evaluation isn't the best option as the student has no prior experience for comparison. Differentiating for some can be tricky. This is partially why I use the end of class as a time for reflection and conversation with the students. I try, for example, to provide important information about how a sore muscle feels different from a sprained muscle and help them to make the best decisions about themselves that they can. By opening up a larger conversation with the entire class, we are able to build a basis for self-evaluation. In other words, we create as a group, a baseline from which future evaluation can be used as a comparison. During this time, I try to delineate a comfort zone, a working zone and an unsafe zone by talking specifically about what actions feel like and how to interpret anatomical or psychological situations. As a complement to this reflective work, I require journaling every class period. I ask the students specific questions about their bodies and their experiences in that class and ask for a one page, typed response where they explore their challenges and successes, their likes and dislikes, and their questions. In this way, they develop a conversation within themselves while simultaneously learning how to write about movement and anatomy using proper vocabulary. I collect these each week so that I have a deeper insight into their experience, which aids in my work with them individually. It's my hope that through these various methods they are guided and encouraged to understand what they are feeling and why. Finally, and maybe most importantly, it is vital that, if there is any question about the health of a student, they are sent to a doctor or physical therapist. I stress clearly to the students that I am neither and do not expect them or me to try to diagnose anything. When in doubt, go see a professional.

PACE

As outlined above, I firmly believe that, in the classroom, students should be assessed with reference to their own growth. In the university, my aerial class is not solely the purview of dance students. Students come to aerial from across a multitude of majors. Some of them are athletes and are interested in the class due to its physical nature. Others have never taken dance and find the subject interesting. Others feel that traditional dance is too specialized and foreign to them and aerial feels more democratic. A small but tenacious group is those that have never danced or played sports and are looking to challenge themselves in a brand new way. Clearly, all of these students have widely varying abilities and experiences. They have different objectives and what each wants to get out of the class is wildly divergent. I find these mixed groups particularly stimulating and find, time after time, that I've learned something new from them. One may think that dancers would make the best natural aerialists, but interestingly, I have not always found that to be true. In my experience, dancers coming out of studio schools have been taught to rely heavily on mirrors. They have learned alignment by watching themselves. By repeating certain movements over and over they learn how it feels to execute a phrase correctly, but often it seems to be a product of memorization, not internal assessment. I've found that if a student doesn't have a sense of alignment through muscle memory or body/mind connection, the lack of mirrors is a huge drawback. In these cases, I have to start from a very elementary place, teaching what proper alignment *feels* like, and slowly work up to even the most basic of aerial exercises. Even for those with a good sense of alignment, when their bodies are placed perpendicular to the way they are used to learning, it's a very challenging situation. There have been times when students with no dance training have been easier to teach. It appears as though this is due to lack of habits that have to be un-learned for aerial. It's sort of like starting from a blank slate. I had a student in the early days of teaching aerial at the university who was remarkable and seemed to naturally know her place in space and move with correct alignment and agility. I shouldn't have been surprised to later learn that she was on the swim team. She was already trained to know where she was in space internally, without having to watch herself. Not only was this helpful in terms of alignment, it contributed to very skilled turns, spins and inverting, all of which are necessary for competitive swimming. Writing about her reminds me of another student who is probably one of the most daring that I've had. He very quickly moved into triple spins (while the class was learning single spins). He was the first in the class to perform a double back flip with an extended body (not an easy task considering he was about was about 6'3" and our rehearsal rig was only twenty five feet high). Excited by the opportunities provided by aerial dance, he trained with a martial arts teacher and choreographed a piece that was vibrant with creativity and virtuosity. While I believe the other students were eventually capable of this advanced work in a technical sense, I think his fearlessness was what set him apart. This boldness (and his adept skills in motion and agility) was a result of his experience in collegiate high jump and triple jump. He applied principles from track & field to aerial and they aided his growth exponentially. Another student took the class with the goal of overcoming debilitating acrophobia. This gave me pause at first because I felt a bit out of my depth. I'm not qualified to aid in this sort of situation but I wanted to support her and help her have a good experience in the class. After discussing my concerns and hers, it was decided that she'd stay in class for a week and I would teach her in the same way as all of the other students. It was agreed that if she couldn't cope for those five days, she'd drop the class. Not only did she stay in the class, she ended up choreographing a solo at the very top of the 40-foot performance wall. She was an amazing combination of bravery and fortitude. Things don't always work out this well as these sorts of personal issues very much depend on the student in question. However, I mention it here along with other examples to illustrate the point that students bring with them advantages and challenges. I feel that it's my job as an educator to accept them as they are and to encourage them to grow. This means every student is working to challenge themselves, not to compare or compete with others in the class. I customize my grading rubric in an effort to record each person's path of growth. In order to do this successfully, I spend time discovering the students' abilities and strengths as well as understanding their personal challenges. I do this as part of the feedback at the end of each class and by reading their daily response journals. In addition to aiding in mapping the growth of each student, learning about their lives can help frame class descriptions or explanations in ways that make sense to them and help them to translate their body knowledge into aerial movement. I believe also that by sharing verbally with everyone in the room, it helps those who are timid by providing a forum through which others can support them, give advice and, as usually happens, friendship.

INJURIES

I was devastated one summer when I had arranged to attend the Aerial Dance Festival in Boulder, CO with an advanced student and ended up hurting my knee a few days before we had planned to leave. It was stupid on my part. The university wanted to do a story on our summer aerial research and I got on the wall to demonstrate for a video they were making without warming up. How stupid was that? If this had been part of a class or if they wanted student footage only, I would have warmed them up, outfitted them correctly and followed all the safety protocols prior to filming. I paid for my sin by having to pull out of an exciting summer of learning and fun. Lesson learned. The takeaway here is that *everyone*, regardless of experience or ability, can be injured. In past chapters I've outlined all the safety measures that are imperative in aerial dance. However, you can do everything perfectly and still be injured. All it takes is returning to the wall with your elbow at a funky angle, pushing away with your ankle not aligned or slamming into the wall on your back because you haven't rotated enough, to produce bruises, sprains, and fractures. These sorts of things must not be handled in-house. I've found that dancers, sometimes so used to taking class with physical injuries, typically try to keep going. I absolutely don't allow this and require them to have a doctor's visit and follow whatever prescription is required. This can be rough on a student when they are taking an intensive class that meets everyday and she will typically feel stressed about missing so much. In this case, don't undervalue the effect on students of watching class. By watching, I actually do mean *actively* watching. (Not doing other work or texting or sleeping.) When I have a student who is injured, I require them to come to class and give them duties that engage them in the class without taxing their injury. There have been times when students have videoed aerial phrases, transcribed my directions for given exercises on a computer, given feedback, or worked on choreography from the ground on choreography from a different perspective. These are all ways to further the education of the aerial student if he is restricted from flying and they serve to keep moving him forward. Then, when the injury is healed and he can return to the wall, he doesn't feel left behind. Every once in a while, a doctor will clear a student to return to aerial practice but indicates a specific part of the body that needs to be kept immobile or not used. Clearly, this is nearly an impossible task. Aerial class isn't for rehab and I can't guarantee that they won't be further injured. I don't allow anyone to get onto the ropes unless they are healthy. There are no guarantees when you are flying 40 feet off of the ground attached to a rope. Better safe than potentially making the injury worse.

ILLNESS

I can't tell you the number of times that students come to class sick. They tend to be concerned about missing class and the effect of non-attendance on their grade, and so make poor decisions regarding their health. It goes without saying that aerial is very taxing. It requires every bit of a person's strength and focus. If, for any reason, a student is compromised, the chance for injury increases dramatically. Head colds wreak havoc in aerial class because the student's equilibrium is usually shot and tipping sideways or upside down shifts all that goop around which makes everything harder. Additionally there are some cold and flu medications that, although they relieve the stuffy head symptoms, can have side effects that make aerial more hazardous. Be wary of any drugs that caution you not to use machinery or drive a car. If you can't drive a car, you can't do aerial. It should go without saying (although I always have to say it to my students) that any sort of nausea does not mix with aerial work. Aerial flipping and turning can be hard enough on one's stomach without other forces at work. When ill in this way, I recommend staying home. The students don't get anything from the class because they feel too poorly to participate in small ways and they, more than likely, will pass on their germs to others. Because some colds and flus take literally a week to get over, in some cases, I have the students lie on the floor and complete what exercises they can while the other students perform the same ones on the wall. Clearly this doesn't work with anything involving flying through space, but the initial floor and wall warm up can be translated fairly well. This at least keeps them moving a bit while they are recovering. As stated earlier, writing or video projects involving the aerial class are good learning tools during recovery. I'm constantly impressed by how much the students learn by watching, even if they can't move their bodies.

Other Essentials

WHAT TO BRING

Clothing

Appropriate clothing is very important in aerial class. Students who've never taken aerial before tend to either dress like they are taking a ballet class in leotard and tights or dress like they are going for a run in shorts and t-shirts. I am very specific about clothing for aerial because it can help or hinder the dancer. I ask my students to wear leggings that are tight and fall below the knee (to the ankle is even better). This helps to protect the skin from abrasions from the wall (especially on brick or concrete) and does not run the risk of getting caught up in the grigri or other equipment and jamming the system and potentially hurting the dancer. For new aerialists, I recommend thick or padded leggings and even layering more than one pair. Any extra padding to the waist, thigh or hip area is a help to the aerialist because the harness can become quite painful. Students like to wear sweat pants because they are generally thick, and while that is a benefit, baggy sweat pants make it difficult for me to see their bodies. I tend to suggest tight sweat pants over full-length leggings for those who desire padding. Men, who tend to be more conscious of their bodies in leggings then women, sometimes ask to wear shorts over their leggings. This is fine for men and women as long as they are not too loose fitting or too long.

The best top for a student aerialist is one that has long sleeves and is long waisted but is tight to the body. This is mainly for protection from the harness, the wall and the rope. If a shirt is worn that doesn't come below the belly button or to the hips, it will gradually ride up above the harness. A harness on bare skin is quite painful. Long sleeves protect the arms of the dancer from the wall and the harshness of the rope. However, the sleeves can't be billowy or it might obstruct the equipment and the top needs to be tight enough so that the teacher can properly see the body. I recommend a leotard underneath the long sleeved shirt so that, should it ride up, the torso is still covered. Layers are good for extra padding as well.

Wool socks or some sort of wicking socks that breathe and appropriate shoes (covered in Equipment, Shoes pp. 9–10) are essential. I mention specific socks because you'll need something that doesn't allow moisture to build up in your shoe. Once you get moisture trapped,

Figure 11.01 Sweatpants may prevent chafing and bruising from the harness
Credit: photo courtesy of Emma Mansfield

you get bacteria which leads to smell. This sort of environment leads to blisters as well. Cotton socks are pretty bad at wicking and tend to get wet and stay wet. Wool is good because in addition to its wicking tendencies, it also absorbs wetness and keeps it away from the feet and its thickness provides nice padding. Merino wool socks are nice because, in addition to the qualities of wool mentioned above, they are inherently antibacterial. There are tons of options out there. Do your research.

Students of aerial tend to sweat so much that some like to bring a shirt to change into after class. This is especially a good idea in the winter. I recommend students also bring a towel. During their down time, they can towel off their faces and hands and some even like to take their shoes off and towel off their feet. (If you think you'd like to do this please don't use one towel for both your feet and your face. Gross.)

Water

This is covered in great detail in Wellness, Water, p. 103 but it's so important that I'm saying it again. **Every student should come to class every day with a water bottle.** (See how I bolded it to show its importance?) I provide water so that the students can have unlimited refills. Drinks with electrolytes are fine as they replace, among other things, potassium and sodium which are necessary for muscle function. (I would stay away from the ones that contain high fructose corn syrup, though) . . . Don't even think of bringing energy drinks or soft drinks to class! In addition to water, during long, intensive classes bring cut fruit or dried fruit and nuts to snack on during down time. (These must be consumed in moderation. You will spin some more.) A little bit of sugar or protein goes a long way toward reenergizing the dancer during an intensive class. Do it. Do it. Do it. If it's a pain, still do it. (Lecture over.)

WHAT TO LEAVE

Jewelry

I feel like I say it every week in every class for the entire semester – leave your jewelry and watches at home. I have to keep saying it though because it's not something that the average student thinks about and usually aerial class is one of twelve thousand things on their minds. Bracelets and watches can easily become damaged as an aerialist flies into a wall. Rings can get caught on the rope and on clothing and either break or rip the skin of the dancer. Necklaces are just plain dangerous. They can get caught up in equipment and either choke the dancer or get ripped off and remove some skin. Jewelry can also potentially damage the equipment if it gets caught up in the mechanisms. I had a student once that almost had an earring ripped straight out of her ear. It was dragged down through her ear lobe. Luckily it broke before it pulled too far through the skin but it was painful. Obviously dangling earrings are a bad idea, but I won't even let my students wear studs. Any sort of body adornment is just an accident waiting to happen. (I once was appalled when teaching an aerial silks class to find that a student had gotten caught in the silk by an ornament in her lower back. I didn't even know she had piercings because she never told me about them. She could have been hurt badly.) In the case of piercings of the body, if they can't remove the ornaments for some reason, they have to wear a leotard. Or, if a leotard won't cover it, they have to bandage it up with tape. This sort of thing needs to be dealt with on a case-by-case basis and you need to encourage your students to be honest with you. It's for their safety after all. When students forget to leave their jewelry at home, it forces me to have to provide a means for storing them in the studio during class. Someone inevitably forgets to take something with them when they leave and, if it gets lost or someone else takes it, is devastated. It could potentially become a liability issue. It's so much easier if everything is just left at home.

Your vanity

One thing that is as dependable as spring turning into summer is there will be students who don't want to look "ugly" (their words not mine) in class. This is usually in reference to the helmets that they have to wear for protection and tends to run to hair issues as well. A rule of thumb in my class is that if I can see their hair peeping out from below or from the sides of the helmet, it has to be secured up inside the hat. Of course everyone hates this rule because they feel ugly. My response? Too bad. That may sound harsh but at the end of the day, the students' safety is the most important thing to me. Back in the day when I rigged the swivel down near the carabiner at the grigri level, we had a few scares with hair getting caught in the turning mechanism. (This, along with clothing getting caught is the reason I moved the swivel.) Even without the swivel in place, the carabiner and the grigri are pieces of metal equipment and stray hairs can easily get caught and ripped out. Similarly, super long bangs or longer sections of hair in the front of the head on men and women have to be pulled back into the helmet. Unobstructed vision is really important for safety. No one should be looking through their hair while they are flying through space. Most of the students fashion a flat sort of bun that keeps the hair up and away but also doesn't take up a ton of space inside the helmet. It's a good idea not to use big metal hair barrettes or bobby pins inside the helmet as they could stick into the scalp in a crash and damage the head and the helmet. Any type of soft ponytail holder or bandana or headband works. I just remind them that wearing a helmet is temporary. They'd be much sadder if they didn't wear the helmet and something permanent scarred their heads or faces.

The Performance

Preparing for an aerial performance is exhilarating. Four months is a short period of time for brand new aerial dance students to make significant progress. However, they grow quite beautifully and evolve into lovely movers with great strength and skill. One of the biggest challenges my students face is in the few days prior to performance, when the height of their rig changes dramatically. Completing a forward walkover, for example, 15 feet below the rig point and performing it 5 feet below the rig point are two very different experiences. Not only are the force and the effort required different, so is the amount of space between the dancer and the vertical surface, as well as the push off and recovery time. I find it very interesting to watch my students as I move them from our rehearsal space, where they have a 20-foot rig point, to our performance space where the rig height reaches a lofty 40 feet. It's very challenging for them because they've arranged their choreography, including shapes and timing based on how they travel through space on a 20-foot rig. With only 2–3 days of rehearsal they have to adjust to a rig that is double the height they are familiar with. Adjustments have to be made so that when the students push off the wall the timing is correct on the return. Part of their challenge is within their own bodies as they push harder or softer to achieve the required results. Another demanding aspect is finding at what point on the 40-foot rope do their phrases most mimic their rehearsal on the shorter rope. I find this process fascinating. It's a conversation within the dancer in relation to his/her new environment.

For these large, outdoor performances, I work with ZFX, a professional rigging company that provides flying effects, custom built equipment, installation and a host of other services. During our four week intensive semester, I work with my dancers inside a black box theatre on campus. This usually consists of a daily rehearsal of 3 hours in the morning, followed by a few hours of rest and to eat lunch and then 3 more hours in the afternoon. After four weeks of this process not only are the dancers strong but they have learned the intricacies and idiosyncracies of their particular ropes and have managed to create a muscle memory related to their height on the rope and the timing of the movements. This allows for their form and the choreography to be reproduced with precision. A great challenge occurs when ZFX arrives. At this point we move from inside to outside. We move from a 20-foot catwalk to a 40-foot wall with the sky as our ceiling. Everything the students learned about motion, timing and force is disrupted. They no longer can walkover two times and then flip with minimal force over an 8 count. They have to alter their internal clock and their

Figure 12.01 Spring term performance
Credit: © Washington and Lee University 2009

proprioceptors, the force verses timing lessons that have become routine are uprooted. It is a huge adjustment that has to happen in a very short period. It is equal parts exciting and terrifying. However, the entire, intense process is made easier by the artists at ZFX. They understand timing. They understand the communicative power of movement, the dynamics of motion, and the fusion of dance and flight. They are artists. Their artistry combined with the very adaptable minds and bodies of the dancers form a collaborative experience, a synthesis. The person who can best describe this partnership is my friend, colleague, and performance rigger, Schu.

The Role of the Flying Director, by Jason Schumacher

Jason Schumacher, originally from Alaska, is the general manager at ZFX, Inc. He's also a professional film producer, stunt coordinator, and actor. He's an ETCP certified arena and theatre rigger, an ETCP recognized trainer, and a member of SAG/AFTRA. He's been charged by a moose, kicked by a horse, and stung by a stingray. He lives in Louisville, Kentucky with his wife and children.

Most performance pieces that demand performer flying, whether they are middle school productions of *Peter Pan*, *Wicked* on Broadway, or the more complicated aerial dance pieces, involve the participation and leadership of a flying director. Often, but not always, these individuals are trained and employed by one of the handful of professional performer flying effects companies scattered throughout the United States and around the world. The job of the flying director is to safely rig the flying systems, choreograph the effect along with the creative team, teach the performers and operators how to execute the choreography, and occasionally operate during the performances.

At ZFX, the flying effects company that I manage, we prioritize the artistic skill set of the flying director just below safety, which is the primary goal of all performer flying effects companies. Our flying directors understand that while the technical aspects of performer flying – ropes, pulleys, harnesses, winches, and all else – are vital to creating the effect of flight on stage, the effect itself is far from the sum of the technical wizardry required to safely lift someone off the ground. Whether the flight is a component of a narrative, as in the many stage plays that require flying, or part of a more conceptual performance, the key to creating effective movement is understanding the physics, biomechanics, and aesthetics of performer flying.

Understanding the physics of aerial movement extends beyond simply grasping the effects of gravity on an object in motion. A skilled flying director synthesizes knowledge of physics with knowledge of a particular flying system to create the desired movement. This takes some rote learning, but also requires active learning on the part of the flying director, who must spend hundreds of hours rigging, operating, and observing the use of flying systems in order to fully grasp how small changes to the system or to the use of the system can affect the movement of the performer. For example, a flying director must understand how extending a pendulum arm two feet will affect the swing of a performer or how adjusting the deceleration rate of a high-speed winch can affect the landing of a performer.

A thorough grasp of the biomechanics of performer flying is vital for choreographing and teaching aerial performance. Performer flying has few analogous movement styles, and there is a completely different relationship with gravity when compared to other physical performance disciplines like dance or stage combat. Even the highest *jeté* requires the dancer to push against the floor, and like all grounded movement it relies on the resistance of earth to propel the performer into the air. When suspended by ropes and a harness, though, the performer has no appreciable resistance from the empty air surrounding them, forcing them to twist, torque, and generally position their body to achieve the movement desired. Flying directors are adept at not only understanding how a performer must manipulate their body to create a desired effect, but they also know how to communicate with performers and to teach them the skills necessary for aerial movement.

Movement aesthetics are, of course, intrinsic to compelling flying effects. Flying directors are, at their core, movement artists who create using the human form as it travels in the air, and much of their training and experience focuses on understanding how to create meaning with the medium. Flying directors must understand the art of storytelling, and understand that an unmotivated flight, no matter how spectacular, will leave the audience feeling unsatisfied and empty. To tell a story, whether it is narrative, interpretive, or conceptual, linear or circular, the flying director must lead the creative team and the performers toward a physical vocabulary that satisfies an audience's need for meaning creation, even when the team has little to no experience with performer flying.

Movement training and choreographic experience outweigh any technical experience when ZFX is hiring flying directors. Technical skills are taught, but true creativity is a process that lives beyond a training program. A flying director must be an accomplished and scrupulously safe rigger, but to get the effects that tell a story and move an audience, the flying director must also be an artist.

———————————

I've been fortunate to witness some beautiful acts of creativity by my students over the years. Once, eight years ago, and another time since, students have experimented with paint and aerial dance. The first performance integrated paint rollers, brushes and various colors of paint. The choreographer worked very hard to use aerial technique as a means of creating images on the wall in paint. She used great sweeping swings to apply long lines of yellow, for example, and inversions to create slashes of blue and red in curves. It was a wonderful exploration in using aerial movement as a source for visual art. She challenged herself in an exciting way to "record" the path of the dance with paint. A few years later, this idea was expounded upon when two dancers using squirt bottles filled with paint, put a canvas on the ground and, as they moved through the air, the movement choices they made caused the paint to release at specific times to create patterns and shapes. Their dance resulted in the capturing of their movement's pathways in a tangible way.

Figure 12.02 Aerial paint
Credit: © Washington and Lee University 2011

There was a fantastic bit of creativity by a student who paired his love of basketball with aerial dance. He created a piece of choreography that incorporated dribbling a basketball up the wall about 40 feet, bouncing it onto the ground (very hard), throwing and catching it while moving through the air tethered to an airline cable. One image that sticks in my mind was when he rotated up, around and down his clip-in point so that he could dribble the basketball in a complete circle. This was immensely hard given that his and the ball's relationship to gravity was shifting the entire time. It was marvelous to watch (see Figure 12.03).

Another beautiful idea that was explored but never made into choreography was actually from a photo shoot. At the suggestion of our photographer, Kevin Remington, we put white paper on the floor, rigged two dancers and hung lighting instruments above them. We gave them a long piece of fabric and asked them to improvise. As they moved through space, creating light and shadow imagines, he took this lovely shot (see Figure 12.04).

As I finish writing about my exploration into rope and harness, about the joys and challenges, I am reminded of when I first broached the subject of exploring flight, well over 15 years ago, to my then board of directors at Roanoke Ballet Theatre. The graciousness of Ann and Bill Hopkins and Maryanne Marx, and the trust of James Sears and our colleagues and partners at Center in the Square, encouraged me to take the risk. All these years later, the things that fascinated me about aerial dance have not changed. Experimentation in motion and the human body bears research for a lifetime. Coupled with the ongoing challenge of discovering new, inventive ways to use the body for expression, it's ever exciting. Aerial dance is quite an apt metaphor for transcending those things that hold us down. It is freedom through movement. It has an ethereal quality that inspires audiences with its beauty and an empowering force that galvanizes the dancer. It can tell a story, celebrate a place, express an emotion or just explore moving through the air. Its democratic nature proves you don't have to be a dancer to be an aerial dancer. True to its modern dance heritage, philosophically, it represents a departure from the norm. An exploration. Aerial is in the process of evolving and growing and its newness means there isn't a canon that can hold it back, nor regulate it. New worlds are being discovered, and boundaries pushed. An integrated community of artists, materials and lessons are shared as we learn from one another. Aerial dance is a collaborative exploration of freedom.

Figure 12.03 Basketball dance
Credit © Washington and Lee University 2009

Figure 12.04 Shadow improvisation
Credit © Washington and Lee University 2009

CHAPTER 13

Philosophies and Advice

I've had the wonderful fortune to work with and learn from amazing aerial dancers and chore-ographers, take part in master classes, and witness gorgeous performances. I've learned throughout these experiences, that the aerial dance community is not only bold, intense, and full of excitement about their art form, they are wonderfully generous individuals. I felt it might be illuminating to hear directly from these artists, who are leading innovators in aerial.

Figure 13.01 Fierce and fearless artists
Credit: © Washington and Lee University 2009

The eclectic collection that follows contain interviews with internationally acclaimed aerial artists, choreographers, teachers, and friends. I spoke with some of them in person and corresponded with others via email to gather their personal stories, insights, and inspirations. Evidence of the generosity of the community is their willingness to share their time with me. I asked all of these artists the same basic questions but I let the interview grow organically based on their responses and followed where the path led. I include below these artists' (in alphabetical order) reflections, ideas, and philosophies on aerial dance. I've been so fortunate to know and learn from these individuals and it's with great pleasure and humility that I include them in this book. They are mavericks. They are ground breaking artists. They are fierce, fearless artists. It It has been such a pleasure working with and getting to know them.

Andrea Chastant Burkholder, Aerialist
Milwaukee, WI

Andrea Chastant Burkholder has been a choreographer, teacher and arts activist for two decades. She performed with Seize the Day! *mixed abilities performance company for 10 years and Andrea founded and ran Washington DC's acclaimed aerial duo company,* Arachne Aerial Arts *for over 10 years, teaching, choreographing and performing aerial arts and collaborating with multi media artists across the country. Some of the many venues she's performed at include the* John F Kennedy Center for the Performing Arts *(DC),* Clarice Smith Center for the Performing Arts *(MD),* Northern Virginia Fine Arts Festival *(VA), and DC's inaugural* Fringe Festival. *She has also been an aerial choreographer for theatre companies in DC, VA and MI. Andrea strives to find ways to allow for open access for the arts, through events such as her* First Friday pay-what-you-will *movement series in Milwaukee,* Real Time. *Andrea teaches aerial workshops and retreats with Susan Murphy, who has taught aerial dance at* University of Wisconsin, Milwaukee *and, as a fully certified pilates practitioner for 16 years, teaches private and group lessons in the Milwaukee area. For more information:* AndreaBurkholder.com

Do you find any issues when dancers are transitioning from traditional dance to aerial?

What I find important is adding aerial dance to the skill set and repertoire of the performer. In this way, there is no "transition" to aerial, but an "addition of" aerial. When working with dancers who have come from a strong physical, partnering base in dance, aerial work seems a natural progression/challenge/inspiration. The apparatus is often like a partner. Full body awareness is key to beautiful, safe and strong aerial work, but I would say that is also true with ground dance. When working with less embodied performers, I have found we need to work on how they relate to the ground and gravity on the floor before working in the air can make sense.

Can you speak to the communicative powers of aerial dance? How do you explore in aerial?

Aerial work is another option in exploring how to express my ideas through my art. I often explain to people that what aerial does is afford me more of the space as usable, so if an alternate or expanded space serves the piece, then I incorporate aerial elements. Also, the apparatus must be considered. Some apparati limit greatly the floor space that you can use, but increase your vertical space, and some allow for easy transition from ground to air so that the entire space is available. Apparati can serve as a prop, a partner, a tool, or a set piece. If I am only able to use one apparatus, I may not have the proper tool for the task at hand. So, I consider seriously which apparatus to use and when an invented apparatus is necessary. In my latest evening-length piece, "Bayou's State", I developed a script from research and personal story and created a nonlinear story using text, dance, and aerial dance. The apparati were danced in and on, and served as images for a set. Three different aerial apparati were used, a low net which had the image of a shrimping net, an inverted bungee apparatus to give the image of the ground sinking away, and a single point trapeze that could be used as a roost above.

Do you feel a strong improvisational education is necessary for aerial?

Once I was in the place to teach my own aerial technique classes, I immediately incorporated improvisation into them. Improvisation teaches the aerialist to pay attention to how they relate to others and to the space. It also teaches you to work with the unknown and variables. In aerial work, the more variables you can accommodate, the safer and more skilled a performer you are.

Do you advocate a plan for optimal conditioning for aerial dance?

If you are only rehearsing, then you are simply maintaining and not growing. Ideally, any performing artist is cross training – taking classes to continue learning, working out to keep up strength and endurance, and studying a somatic practice (like pilates, yoga, Feldenkrais) to continue to integrate their body.

How does aerial contribute to the modern dance canon?

In the dance world, genres are being blended to create the piece that the artist needs to create. Many artists are adding aerial work to their theater and dance pieces without actually creating an "aerial dance". Aerial is another addition into "Contemporary Performance" and in this way has added breadth to the modern dance canon.

What is your approach to teaching aerial?

After teaching private aerial lessons for many years, I began teaching an aerial technique class based on my many years as a modern dancer, because I saw the need for aerialists to become more embodied. I created a series of ground-based warm ups with themes of body connectivity and conditioning. I would always teach them an aerial phrase that would continue to build into a whole dance, and each class ended with improvisational scores that fit the theme of the phrase and skills needed to be able to perform more fully.

Do you consider aerial a reframing of traditional dance forms?

No, aerial is not a reframing of traditional dance forms. It has its own integrity and techniques, and blends beautifully in with any dance form.

Do you feel pressure to try to "fit" aerial into the dance continuum?

No. After paving the way with Sharon Witting in Arachne Aerial Arts to create a new way to create aerial partnering, I have allowed my interests to define how I use my skills in each piece I create. My creations lie somewhere in the realm of contemporary performance, as they are always movement based, but can be considered theatrical as well. So many performing artists are choosing this path that we all fit into the continuum because part of the continuum is carving your own way.

What advice would you give aspiring college students who want to be aerial dancers?

Be physical. Dare to dive in and explore aerial work – its great physicality, and its ability to transform. Allow yourself the time to investigate aerial as an art form, and honor the techniques that teach proper alignment, safety and form. Learn basic skills and techniques so that you can avoid injuries and have a base from which to work.

———————————

Joanna Haigood, Zaccho Dance Theatre
San Francisco, CA

Since 1979 Joanna has been creating work that uses natural, architectural and cultural environments as points of departure for movement exploration and narrative. Her stages have included grain terminals, a clock tower, the pope's palace, military forts, and a mile of urban neighborhood streets in the South Bronx. Her work has been commissioned by many arts institutions, including Dancing in the Streets, Jacob's Pillow Dance Festival, Walker Arts Center, *the* Exploratorium Museum, the National Black Arts Festival, *and* Festival d'Avignon. *She has also been honored with the* Guggenheim Fellowship, *the* Cal/Alpert Award in Dance, *the* US Artist Fellowship, *and a* New York Bessie Award. *Most recently, Haigood was a recipient of the esteemed* Doris Duke Performing Artist Award. *Joanna has had the privilege to mentor many extraordinary young artists internationally at the* National École des Arts du Cirque *in France, the* Trinity Laban Conservatoire of Music and Dance *in England,* Spelman College, *the* Institute for Diversity in the Arts at Stanford University, *the* San Francisco Circus Center *and at* Zaccho Studio.

Her company, Zaccho Dance Theatre, *makes its home in San Francisco's* Bayview Hunters Point. *Zaccho manages a studio that is utilized for rehearsal, performances, artist residencies, and educational activities for youth and adults.* www.zaccho.org

How do you feel about the legitimization of aerial?

In many respects the form *has* been legitimized in the last ten years. When I started, which was in the late 70s, there were dancers already exploring aerial work. Trisha Brown had been incorporating aerial elements into her work for some time. Also Stephanie Evanitsky created a company, Mulitgravitational Aerodance, that was focused primarily on aerial dance. But what we are seeing now is different. It really is a new genre. It wasn't exactly a "genre" then. Dancers were using aerial tools to move the body into different areas of the space or environment, studies in inversion, studies in time. It was very difficult to get funding early on because it wasn't considered "dance". It was considered acrobatics or circus, even though the circus community certainly didn't see it as such. Back then, there wasn't as much cross training. That is not the case now. There is much more cross training. Circus incorporates theater and dance and aerial dancers train in high level aerial techniques.

It has been said that aerial is reframing traditional dance forms and innovating with new challenges and freedoms. I wonder how you feel those innovations shape the art form? Or, are in the process of shaping it?

There are many different ways that choreographers use aerial techniques. Some use them to explore the body and movement vocabularies in relationship to an (aerial) object, like a trapeze, a ladder and chair. Then there are those, like me, who are also interested in shaping the space using aerial rigging and techniques to engage the space more "sculpturally". There are choreographers that are using dance vocabulary on the ground and making the transition into the air quite beautifully.

Do you consider yourself a conceptual artist or do you work more architecturally? Are there degrees of integration?

I consider myself a site artist primarily, although I have been making more theater work in the last few years. I use the aerial work to describe the various elements and characteristics of the site. That includes the nuances of the site or place, in general. I think about how to charge the space in a different way and how to use it poetically. The site itself, its history and its potential for metaphor, and the ability to explore it in a more expansive way inspires/informs so much of my work.

I assume, when you are making a site-specific work, that you generally can't rehearse in the performance space for weeks at a time. How do you handle that?

There is a lot to consider when you are working on a large-scale project, like the airport, for example. We make field studies, observe the general activity, the sound, light, weather, etc.; we take measurements, I try to estimate the timing – how long it takes to get from point A to point B. Sometimes I have to find alternative spaces that can replicate some of the elements of the site we are performing in. When I was creating the piece for grain elevators in New York and Minneapolis, I used a cargo crane at the SF Port so I could work with a similar rope length. But what I couldn't measure until we rehearsed at the site was the climbing of 12 flights of stairs, which impacted the timing *and* the energy of the dancers. We did train for this but it was difficult to know exactly. We also had a last-minute change where the dancers were required to climb a 110 foot vertical ladder to get to the roof. That was a huge challenge but it was met by the dancers with great enthusiasm. They are extraordinary. I try my best to get as much time as I can on site. If I'm lucky, I can negotiate for two weeks but usually it's about eight to ten days. It's just enough to sew the parts together.

Can you talk about the dancers in your company? What sort of training do they have?

They are brilliant artists and thinkers and bring a great deal to the process. Most of them are dancers who have some gymnastics and/or aerial training. There are also some who come from circus and have skills in various forms. There is a lot of skill sharing among the dancers. What I'm working on now is getting performers to cross train so the skills are more balanced. Many of them are directors and choreographers of their own work so have a great deal of knowledge of the creation process.

Do you feel that the doing is the training?

Some of it is. Some of the projects require the dancers to learn new skills. But there are basics that need to be learned and mastered, things that apply to many of the challenges that need to be met in the projects. Just as a ballet dancer must master the plié or a pirouette, we must master the basics of climbing, integration with a moving object, standing on a wall in a harness.

I've found that the differences in training are apparent, for example, between dancers and athletes. Swimmers, for instance, have developed through swimming an awareness of the three-dimensionality of space but dancers, those who maybe used mirrors in class, may have no frame of reference for their bodies in space. Clearly, dancers have the technique needed for aerial dance but in other ways they may be limited because they've never worked in this specific way in a 3-dimensional world.

Yes, plus there is the issue of being inverted, which I think is very difficult for some people. It can be very disorientating and very difficult to execute basic choreography. Sometimes people have uncomfortable physical responses, like dizziness and nausea. That's usually the thing that I come across with students at the beginning. I do love teaching dancers. They are deeply aware of their bodies and can translate skills very quickly.

Do you use a lot of improvisation? Do you expect your dancers to contribute?

Yes, always. I set up problems and then the dancers improvise. Today we did improvisations being pulled up the ladder as opposed to climbing. Everyone has a different interpretation of what that is. Through the improvisation you can see the elements that illustrate the idea that you are working toward. Sometimes I have no idea what I am looking for until I see something that inspires me. Then a door opens and I can begin to explore.

Is that what keeps it exciting for you?

Yes, plus that I work with brilliant dancers. They are amazing. Not just great. They are super great! They keep investing in the process, which I am grateful for. They know in the end, I may change things or manipulate things or throw away things but that's part of our agreement. They trust me to lead them through a process of learning and growth.

That takes a well trained dancer.

All of the dancers come from rigorous training programs. They have had to be proficient in many styles and techniques. So much of my work asks the dancer to be comfortable with being vulnerable. It requires so much trust . . . everyone supports one another. It is important for me to feature the dancers as individuals – they each bring a unique perspective to the work. I feel that a lot of the process is about creating an effective dialogue with the dancers, which is, I believe, more satisfying for all of us.

Does your company take traditional classes as well?

Yes. All of the dancers are involved in some type of training, be that in dance, theater or in circus aerial skills. In rehearsal, everyone has a different warm up. Occasionally we'll have a company class but not as a rule.

How many are in your company?

12–15. There is a different number and different dancers in each project depending on the needs.

When you all perform rope and harness, do you have custom made harnesses or do you use climbing harnesses?

We do both. We've had custom harnesses made, usually when we want to achieve certain effects. We've also used climbing harnesses and stunt harnesses. Harnesses can be very expensive so that's a big consideration when making the work.

Do you rig your studio for rope and harness to prepare for a concert?

The studio isn't always high enough but we do have lines rigged to do develop wall work. Our ceiling is only 22 feet, so not ideal. 35–40 feet would be a lot better for training.

You must have amazing riggers.

Yes, one of them is my husband, Wayne Campbell. It works out nicely. *laughs* We had an interesting challenge recently, at Ann Hamilton's beautiful tower at Oliver Ranch in Geyserville. It is an 80 foot concrete cylinder with staircases built in a double helix. I wanted the dancer to start on the ground and be pulled up in a way that she circumnavigated the exterior of the building – creating a spiral, candy cane pattern as she ascended. Because this was a highly resonant structure (something Ann intended), I wanted the rigging to be particularly quiet. There were many constraints that made the design process challenging. But after a long "not possible" period, Wayne woke up in the middle of the night with the idea that worked. He created and installed, with the help of our brilliant rigging team (Sean Riley, Dave Freitag and Spencer Evans), an ingenious counterweight system. Silent, effective and visually stunning. Without the riggers, their design and technical expertise, my vision would be limited, to say the least.

It is brilliant in its simplicity.

And in many ways, it was very old fashioned. In earlier days, most theatrical effects were done without machines. They were done with counterweight systems, similar to this one, human power . . . and they were very effective. It is very much like a dance for the riggers as well. Frankly, the rigging choreography is sometimes just as interesting as the "onstage" performance!

This part of the country is fruitful with aerial artists.

I don't know how we all got here but it's fabulous! Terry Sendgraff has been a tremendous inspiration to all of us. She's an extraordinary force of nature. She is attributed with the invention of the low-flying, single point trapeze and her technique, *Motivity*. *Motivity* is an improvisation based technique that explores dancing on the ground and in the air and one where the dancers tap deeply into their emotions, their spirits, and their connection to others and the world around them. In aerial dance, you become very familiar with negotiating with your fear, you work with trust. It pushes you out of your comfort zone. Terry's work does this in such a powerful way, and it is really beautiful to witness. And then there is the wonderful and adventurous Amelia Rudolph. She was a dancer with very strong ties to the climbing community and with a great love for nature. I met her through my husband Wayne, who is also climber. Artist and activist Jo Kreiter came to dance from gymnastics and then to aerial dance. We worked together (she performed in my company) for 13 years before she started her fantastic company, Flyaway Productions. Then there were all the wonderful artists from the circus community, like Wendy Parkman from the Pickle Family Circus and at Circus Center, where I worked for six years. I learned so much there. Each of these artists, among others, and their collaborators have trained so many people in the Bay Area, and those who then went on to build their own work. I think this has attracted many other artists from other parts of the country to come here to study and to start careers. Dancing off the ground is an ancient form and has been practiced all over the world in different ways. An astonishing example is the dance of "Los Voladores" ("The Flyers") from Veracruz, Mexico. I believe this dance is about 400 years old. I saw it in Mexico City about 20 years ago. It is spectacular. The dance involves five men and a thirty-foot pole. They climb up to the top, four dancers tie ropes around their waists, one stands on the top of the pole playing a flute and dancing. The rope slowly unwinds on a spool and the dancers slowly lower to the ground, head first. They transition from one beautiful shape to another as they descend. The most common interpretation is that it is a blessing of the land for fertile ground, rains, and for ending drought. You watch the dancers magically float against the sky for a long time. It's otherworldly and truly remarkable.

[*Note*: The ceremony was named an *intangible cultural heritage* by UNESCO in order to help the ritual thrive and survive in the modern world.]

––––––––––––––

Wendy Hesketh-Ogilvie, Artistic Director, Wired Aerial Theatre
Liverpool, England

Wendy is and has been a highly physical and committed performer since the moment she found balance. An accomplished harness specialist whose focus is channeled towards physical, visceral performance. She is an improviser, a creative, with experience that spans physical theatre, aerial stunts, contemporary dance, percussion, and all kinds of weird and wonderful morphs of skills invented and perfected along her way. She is particularly interested in the subtleties of theatricality within dance performance, and the fusion of dance with harness skills and how aerial work can enhance dance themes/narratives. She is a self-confessed perfectionist, never tiring refining aerial techniques both in performance and in training the body to deal with its complexities. Although she is a harness specialist company, in 1999 she developed an aerial dance technique called bungee-assisted dance and has been continually refining and perfecting vertical wall work in counterbalance. Working with companies such as De La Guarda, Motionhouse, Dream Engine and Scarabeus has influenced her personal journey to transition her to where she is today. As Artistic Director of Wired her focus shifts constantly between performing and directing, designing and delivering physical tuition, writing and researching. Her feet itch and so she moves forwards, thinking that in doing so it may inspire people to follow. Wendy says, "just thinking of how aerial work has affected my life brings me to tears even now – if there is a reason for 'being', this is mine".

What is your dancers' background in training? How do they transition to aerial?

As a company, we work mainly with two aerial harness techniques. We choose to specialize in these and ensure that the feeling and sensation of dance is always in the forefront of what and how we move. These techniques are bungee-assisted dance and vertical wall work. Both techniques involve the wearing of different harnesses with different connection points, one at the front of the body and the other at the back. The aerial performers we work with are always contemporary dance trained. As a trained contemporary dancer myself (having begun working in the air with De La Guarda many moons ago), I recognized how the refined ground based dance techniques my body possessed, enabled me to feel and/or find, exactly the same physical sensations when working in the air. I really enjoy watching dancers move from ground into the air and back again, as well as continual suspended movement and when I train our dancers to work in the air I do so by focusing their attention on how they can retain those ground-based physical sensations when their feet have little or no connection to the floor. We spend a lot of time focusing on how the brain and body responds automatically to these sensations of lift and suspension, and make decisions on whether we work with or against them physically. When working on a vertical surface I work on the basis of, if you can transfer the feeling/ sensation of correct posture and alignment (from the usual vertical position into the 90 degree angle), then all you need to do is be able to use your newly built strength to stay in this plane for longer. I teach ground-based dance exercises on vertical surfaces as part of training as our dancers are most used to performing these. We push through the feet to stand, roll up the spine, bring awareness to our sternum and shoulders etc. etc., pretty much all exercises work in the same way, using this understanding. We use video play back a lot and find it very useful; being in the air makes us feel so amazing that sometimes we believe we are doing something far better than we are because it feels so nice! Cheeky endorphins bring this confusion with them! I give a tremendous amount of feedback to our performers and when looking to clarify body form or execution of skills and technique I use standard physical terms but also sensory approaches too. It has always been important to me to be able to close my eyes and know what my body is doing and how it is lining up. Visualizing our vertical surface as our floor is of upmost importance, to bring freedom and ease to our work, so we work visualization tasks in addition to proprioception exercises really. Of course the only way to be able to freely investigate and relax into this kind of work is to build the appropriate strength and stamina to allow your mind to over power the physical work going on in your body. As our way of knowing if our body is working as we want it to, and to check our body form and timing, we also have installed mirrors in our aerial studio that allow us to see ourselves working on the vertical wall when in the lower heights. A real treat for vertical wall performers!

Can you speak to the communicative powers of aerial dance?

I always say that taking the feet off the ground allows for incredible things to happen. Both from a performer's experience but also from an audience member's experience too. I strongly believe there is a powerful connection you sense when seeing this action or feeling this action happen. This feeling is connected to your heart and we all know how powerful this can be. When the heart is open there is no end to what effects or sensations this can cause.

Explain how you explore content in performance.

I took a really interesting workshop with the amazing Keith Hennessey a long while ago. His approach to using aerial equipment was refreshing. All the things he highlighted were in tune with my thinking and it was joyous to see him bring meaning to aerial work and vise versa. I enjoy the thought that the use of aerial work is there to benefit or enhance the performance piece. We begin by defining in general what we are making; be it a piece of aerial theatre, aerial dance theatre, aerial dance . . . this helps us to stay focused. I'm not sure we always stick to these areas but sometimes when we are undoubtedly working through a creative process, coming back to our area brings some clarity.

Do you feel a strong improvisational education is necessary for aerial?

Sometimes . . . it depends on the type of choreography you are creating. If you wish for clinical vocabulary then possibly you don't need as much of an improvisational approach. However there is nothing better than having the physical strength to play within the parameters afforded to you in each rigging set up, to discover movements and ways of moving that you perhaps haven't tried before. To fully improvise you do need a lot of strength and this is why we provide such in depth and intensive training to all of our chosen performers.

What role does fear play?

I believe that fear is an honest response and this is why I train our performers' brains so much from the beginning. A feeling of fear is real, it is how we work with it to refrain the sensation of fear from entering our body and affecting our physical form. In order to reduce fear (especially when working high) it is important you trust every aspect of your aerial system from your harness (and how you put it on), right through to trusting the equipment and how it is rigged and your assigned counter-balancer who will be on the other end of your rope. I have spent my life working hard to resist the urge to throw myself off balconies and roof tops so although I don't necessarily feel fear, I work with it in a different way. We have a very experienced technical team (we call them climbers) and from the very beginning, when people begin to work with us, we begin to build a relationship of confidence between performer and climber. We always make sure that methods and processes are fully described to all people involved in our work so that we have one way and only that way of working, and everyone knows and understands why it is like that. I take great comfort in feeling that there is a very simple and unified way of working, when working at great heights, following a system really helps you to focus.

What does a typical day look like for your dancers?

As dancers by trade we begin all our days with a ground-based dance class. Exercises are designed to work our body in a way that is conducive to working in the air in whatever technique we will be working with that day. We have developed and refined these exercises over 17 years and believe that this has enabled all our performers to work safely, intelligently and for as long as they wish with little or no injury for as long as they wish.

Do you feel that rehearsing for aerial is enough to prepare you for aerial? Or do you advocate a plan for optimal conditioning?

I use a refined regime of ground-based exercises and vocabulary to prepare my performers to work in the air, as well as aerial exercises and tasks to prepare them fully and appropriately for working in the air for periods of time.

What do your dancers need to bring to the table? How do they contribute?

I love to see how individual performers move when in the air. Different performers have different flavored moves and ways of moving. I like to explore how we can cross-pollinate these things across our company members. I require all of our performers to be able to perform the same way technically, the movements we have in our repertoire, and from this point we can begin to create some pretty amazing vocabulary. I encourage all members to be able to repeat any movement they create so that they are able to teach it to another person. This also embeds the technique in their body while following this process.

Talk about the rigors of aerial from an equipment standpoint.

Jamie (my husband) designed our performance bungee-assisted dance harnesses and we have them fabricated for us. We presently use specific climbing harnesses for our vertical wall work.

What is your approach to teaching?

Yes, bungee-assisted dance is our beloved creation. I have noted the technique from its conception in 1999 to now – an ever-evolving technique, now used globally. More recently we have developed this to fit within the fitness industry. There is absolutely a structure to learning the techniques, and then it becomes super exciting when you begin to work with your skills to create work.

Is your work characteristically more architectural or more conceptual?

This completely depends on whether our work is a commission or if we are creating a performance piece ourselves. Our company works between both. We cross art forms quite a bit, especially with our outdoor large-scale show, *as the world tipped* (a wired aerial theatre production, director: Nigel Jamieson).

Who is your mentor?

I always find this one a little hard. I have loved working with and learning from Nigel Jamieson, we have a very good working relationship. Other than Nigel, I take inspiration and guidance from people who may not be related to aerial work at all. Theatre directors and dance practitioners.

Do you consider aerial a reframing of traditional dance forms?

I see aerial performance as a development of performance forms. An opportunity to use the air and height as a way of expanding possibilities of how we can move and express ourselves overall.

What is your definition of aerial dance?

I have been working on this definition for many years and of course it changes regularly. It is always a work in progress. Sometimes a new thought on how I would define aerial dance shwooshes past my eyes when I am working in the air and I think, ah yes, that is a clearer way of defining this! . . . I believe that aerial dance happens in the air (whether this means on a vertical wall or for moments attached to a bungee, or any other aerial equipment), and that it has an original/recognized ground-based dance form within it. The "aerial" part of the term is easy, it's the "dance" bit that always brings confusion to me. And so I carry on being open and waiting for the next moment of inspiration when I alter my thoughts slightly. The main thing for me is that we can all engage in discussion about this question, as in doing so it allows us to develop vocabulary and a voice and this will strengthen its relevance and positioning across the dance and performance world. Aerial dance/performance brings with it a kind of intrigue that engages people and the public in a refreshing way. Aerial work outdoors seems to have a site-specific element to it and this raises awareness too. When using aerial work in theatres I believe it allows you to explore the regions of the performance stage that are less frequented (this is a common view). In reaching these spaces it unlocks a little vacant space in most people's heads, and allows you to fill it with some pretty special thoughts, images, and possibilities. I'm thrilled that this exists in the dance world. To keep people engaged and interested it is important to keep exploring and developing, sharing and talking.

Do you feel pressure to try to "fit" aerial into the dance continuum?

I don't feel pressure to fit in. As a dancer who moves with this in my bones and brain, it is a given that the work I am drawn to and wish to create will always be rooted in dance. Using aerial work in what we do ultimately brings itself into the dance continuum. It always surprises me to hear that someone believes our work to be circus, but I see it more as having another house we can reside in rather than anything else.

What advice would you give aspiring college students who want to be aerial dancers?

Make friends with the floor, everything moves from this point and this grounding. You must have a real sense of how your weight works in relation to the ground to really get a sense of how this can be lifted in any plane when the feet leave the floor. Make sure you are fully aware of the incredibly vital moment when your feet leave the floor and when they return, this detail allows you to move seamlessly between ground and air and if you focus on the same things that I do, then this is so important for creating the illusion of making the equipment disappear and allowing the audience to focus on the physical body moving in space. Develop your proprioception skills. Train hard and correctly, as strength and stamina will unlock your ability to play and experiment with ease while in the air. Be friendly, inquisitive and focused. The aerial world is small and we need to be a strong family of friends. Don't have a big lunch before working on a vertical wall!!!

Amelia Rudolph, Artistic Director, BANDALOOP
Oakland, CA

Amelia is a choreographer, community leader and dancer/athlete. Her work is informed by aesthetics, non-traditional relationships with gravity, ecology, natural and built spaces, community and human relationships. She founded BANDALOOP *in 1991, bringing together dance, climbing and varied off-the-ground movement through site-reactive work on cliffs, urban structures and in theaters. She is a co-leader for* Creative Capital's Professional Development Program, *teaches youth in* Oakland *through* Destiny Art Center, *is an active and dynamic performer, and serves on the board of* Dance USA. *Amelia holds Bachelors and Masters degrees in comparative religion from Swarthmore College and the Graduate Theological Union, Berkeley. Her intellectual and artistic sensibilities inform her work inspiring practical, spiritual, theoretical and political creativity. Her choreography has explored dance in theaters and on buildings and cliffs all over the US and around the world. Amelia is continually challenged and inspired by her experiences in nature, with her dancers and with communities that unearth and clarify her values, identity, and art. Since 2000 she has been named an* Irvine Fellow *and awarded funding and commissions from the* National Dance Project, Creative Capital, National Performance Network, the National Endowment for the Arts, The Creative Work Fund, San Francisco Foundation, the Irvine Creation to Performance Program, City of Oakland, the* Zellerbach Family Foundation, *and* The Center for Cultural Innovation *among others. In 2009 she received a major commission with* Aeriosa *from the* Arts Partners in Creative Development in Canada *as part of the* Cultural Olympiad. *In 2010–11 the company was awarded major grants from the* Rainin, Wattis and Irvine Foundations *as well as the* San Francisco Arts Commission, *for new work for* BANDALOOP*'s 20th anniversary season in 2011.* BANDALOOP *is a multi-year grant recipient for organizational support from the* William and Flora Hewlett Foundation.

How do you define the aerial dance form?

When people say aerial dance a lot of different things come to mind. For many people what comes to mind is tissue, trapeze and circus-based aerial arts. There is a whole world of dance artisans, of different configurations, that allows dance that comes out of the dance world – ballet, contemporary, modern, post modern dance – to get into the air in some way or the other. In my opinion, they are actually quite different and it's a worthy cause to really be clear about the difference.

What do you consider to be optimal conditioning for aerial dance?

We had to train some performers recently who had to learn how to do pretty hard vertical dance (dancing on a wall in a harness). We had to develop a whole conditioning series of exercises for them to do. I worked on it with one of my alumnus dancers, Mark Stuver. He is really into conditioning and he worked on very specific things to do both in the harness and not in the harness. We asked ourselves, "What parts of your body need to be strong?" Obviously your core, your deep core, your lower abs. Crunches are not going to do it. Do simple planks, elbow planks, side planks, anything that allows your whole body to coordinate in one piece is super important. Any kind of exercises that will lift your hips off the ground, as well as ones that raise both your tailbone and your upper body off the ground at the same time. You need to work the whole length of the core, not just the upper core. Your neck has to be strong. If I haven't done aerial in a few months, that's where I feel it first. It's a funny thing to strengthen and it's actually kind of tricky. There are ways of doing it using machines in the gym. I also use the gym machines to strengthen my lower back. I'm not a big advocate of many repetitions. I believe you should get into position, be still and then move your body like you might as a dancer. That's what I do in the gym. One of the core principles of BANDALOOP technique is called "held core – released distal edges". This means that as a dancer you want to be soft in arms but it takes so much strength that you have to learn how to have a deep strength in your lower abs and even release in your neck so that all the distal parts of you can be soft and moving. This is so important so you train yourself even in the conditioning to hold onto your dancer sensibility and kinetic and kinesthetic sensitivity. I think handstands are really important, as is hanging from your knees but simply being upside down and getting your circulatory system used to being upside down is really important. If I haven't been rehearsing and especially if we're doing hanging work, the first two rehearsals everyone is like *scream*. But your body acclimatizes. Mobilization of spine, which dancers do anyway, is important. We do one exercise where we lie on our stomach and we pull the shoulder blades and legs off the ground, and hold. That builds back core strength. And then roll to the side with back, sides and stomach in control, then roll to the front and side again and hold. This is activating all the muscles you will need when you are in the air.

I've spoken to a lot of people who have professional aerial companies and you're one of the few people who has said you have a conditioning system or technique in place. Mostly everyone says you learn it by doing it.

This is true, you do. But if someone is preparing to do this who is literally not trained in dance, it is different. We have thought about preparing people for aerial because we've had to train corporate and non-profit groups as part of the "BANDALOOP Experience". So we send them these videos we've made that offer varying levels of exercises that prepare the body for aerial work. You're going to have more fun in the workshop if you prepare by doing these exercises first. For example, Disney partnered with a Japanese company for a new show for Disneyland Tokyo. I was hired to choreograph, and this show has a piece in it where two characters end up on this lake and the lake becomes vertical and they dance on it. They asked me to train three pairs of very capable athletic dancer young people how to do what we do in two weeks. I said, I can't do that at the level you want them to perform in two weeks. However, if you have them training for several months before I get there, I can do it. They said, "Great! Send us a training video". So I did and it worked.

Do most of your dancers come from the dance world?

All of them.

Have they studied aerial prior to coming to you?

What's happening now is that dancers are taking our BANDALOOP workshops and getting excited about what we do. My most recent audition, I hired aerialists who had attended those workshops. But, dancers first. Always.

Do you find that when a dancer shifts from dancing to aerial that there are elements that are challenging to them?

There is a learning curve. Even remembering choreography when you're turned sideways on a building is difficult. It's totally different. When you're handing upside down and someone tells you to move your left arm, you don't know what to do. Although I have super strict traditional dance training, I've had enough contract improv experiences to be an advocate of covering mirrors. This is for many reasons including the tendency for dancers to stare at themselves instead of feeling what they're doing. I think it's very valuable to know your alignment without looking at it. I do this thing with dancers where I stand them on the wall sideways and I give them feedback or take pictures of them so they know what to work on. Becoming aware of what you just did is helpful. For new aerialists, learning to go into your backspace is challenging. It's hard enough on the ground. Running backwards is hard. We go into our backspaces as much as we go into forward or sides spaces. That's huge. How do you get accustomed to going that way when you can't see it? I suspect you could consciously articulate that, talk about it and take measures and simply practice those skills. Re-understanding your alignment is so different because the musculature you use to do it is just so different. There are complex issues like how not to use too much energy, how to conserve and be efficient with energy so that you can have enough for the dance. It's different; so different. Footwork is so different. We're used to having all our weight to tell our feet how to be articulate. People can get really sloppy on the wall. You have to rethink and make the dancer conscious of what they are doing because everything that touches the wall is so different then when it's on the ground. You can see it – every landing, every take off, everything. Understanding how to send your energy into your light feet is different. I think you have to be really particular and intentional about how you use that connection.

Do you play with improvisation?

All the time.

So the dancers contribute?

We are very collaborative.

I assume that quality is very valuable when looking for new aerial dancers. The ability to contribute isn't a skill that every dancer possesses. If you've never been given the opportunity to contribute, you've never learned how to.

Absolutely. Frankly, I won't work with a dancer who can't. They'd have to train to be able to learn how to do that and it takes years. Some people are certainly more talented in that respect than others but I have mature dancers. One of the things I appreciate is articulateness in the body. I call it physical intelligence. Being articulate. I look for dancers who are extremely capable and have a wide range and capacity to make choices in space.

They have a voice.

Yes.

Your work seems to be a lot about place. When you make work, is it an architectural exploration of the space you are in or is it more concept based?

It varies. In general I start with an idea. I have become more narrative over the years. Despite the fact that I never really liked Merce Cunningham's work, I have huge intellectual respect for him. I loved Trisha Brown's work. I loved her work. I was one of her official "man walking" people. I am old enough to come from that world – I'm just picking two icons – so I've never had the feeling that I need to tell a specific story. We're going to the mountains next week to film, there are two things going on. One is adaptive choreography to that space. I am repositioning it and adapting it so that it is being completely translated by and into that new space. We won't really know till we get there what is possible and what's not possible and how it can change. That's really fun. I like doing that. For the work that we're adapting, we do a lot of phrase work on the ground and we translate it and adapt it to the wall. I feel like dancers think differently on the ground. We do some of that. Some of it is built on the wall. I often have images and core ideas and will sometimes do timed writing to get people involved in ideas and images. The second thing that's going on is the piece "Coyote Waltzes". There is a basic idea that has to do with our waltz with nature and natural spaces, our dance with nature and using the coyote as a trickster, a teacher, who is the witness to the piece that we are doing. It's filmed from the coyote's perspective. It's about this idea that we're separate and incongruous to these environments and slowly throughout the piece we become more animal-like and more part of the space we're in. That's for the film, not the dance, but it's not unlike how I would make a dance.

How long do you get in the space?

Two days.

That must be a massive undertaking.

To be a dancer, you have to deal with short amounts of time and very difficult situations sometimes. Other times it's perfect. One of the skills it takes to be in this company is the ability to relax and deal with chaos and change and adapting fast. For this film we will take the choreography we are working on today, we will film them right at the beginning and we will have two rehearsals to adapt it, maybe three. This is why you have to adapt. There is no time to show up and make something there. I did it once, in Italy, when we actually made work at the site. We had enough time, but enough time wasn't enough. We had eight days to adapt really quickly and manage and remember all the changes. It is a big skill. This is not one of those companies where you do "that" piece again the same way. You might do that piece again in the "Cleveland version" minus the "North Carolina jumps". You have to remember what version you are on.

What about the varying heights of the buildings when on tour?

The taller the building, the slower the piece. If you have a live musician you can get them to play it slower, which helps. Taller the building, the longer the ropes, the slower the dance, the bigger the jumps. We cut choreography. The shorter the building, the shorter time, the more choreography. We are adapting all the time.

It's a mathematical puzzle.

Yes. We didn't talk about safety, which is the first and most important thing. We have a huge culture of safety and philosophy which has to do with the idea that "nobody's in charge out here". We have experts in the sense that people are extremely good at rigging but, the expert doesn't tell you how it is. You are responsible to understand how it is and if anything doesn't look right, no matter what it is, you ask. You stop and ask for explanation. Everybody matters. Everybody is responsible. There is no hierarchy. Everyone is encouraged to speak up. I believe in safety. Everyone makes mistakes. They make them so you need safety systems that catch them.

More eyes on them.

Yes, and multiple checks and balances.

———————————

Terry Sendgraff, Creator, Motivity
Oakland, CA

Terry Sendgraff is a visionary choreographer, performing artist, and master teacher. She is a noted pioneer of aerial dance and the creator of Motivity, her innovative dance creation and performance style. In 1971, when Terry Sendgraff moved to California, there was no such thing as "aerial dance". In 1975, on the eve of her 42nd birthday, Terry introduced Motivity, and over the course of that decade, aerial dance emerged as a popular post modern dance genre. She obtained a bachelor's degree in Recreation from Pennsylvania State University (1955), and holds a master's degree in Dance from the University of Colorado at Boulder (1969), as well as a master's degree in Clinical Psychology from John F. Kennedy University (1986). In addition, Terry has extensive training in modern dance, ballet, gymnastics, and awareness oriented dance/movement forms. She has created over two hundred concerts, including her unprecedented A Year of Sundays *(1977–1978) and her celebrated* birthday performances *(1974–1983). From 1978–1980 she founded and led* Fly By Nite, *the first women's trapeze dancing troupe in the country; it gave sold-out performances at the* Motivity Center *in Berkeley. From 1991–1994 she founded and directed* Women Walking Tall *stilting troupe for the purpose of empowering women and girls of diverse economic and cultural backgrounds. She established her* Motivity Company *in 1980. She has collaborated with many* Bay Area *performing artists and companies, including Anne Bleuthenthal, Kim Epifano, Shakiri, Wendy Diamond, Al Wunder, Gwen Jones, Dance Brigade,* AXIS Dance Company, *and* Run for Your Life Dance Company. *Terry was a featured artist and faculty member at the* Annual International Aerial Dance Festival *in Boulder, Colorado (1999–2005). She received two* Isadora Duncan Awards: Sustained Achievement *(2005) and* Solo Performance *(1989). In 1989,* PBS *aired* Can You See Me Flying: a Portrait of Terry Sendgraff, *a documentary film by Fawn Yacker. Terry retired in 2005 and is currently writing a book about her life.*

I've found at the university that aerial dance is very exciting to a cross section of students. They love it and want to do it, regardless of their movement experience.

Well, yes. It's such a great feeling. It's a way to fly. Rope and harness is free. The legs are free and the arms are free. You're just held up and you're off the ground, and that's a new experience. It's a new proprioceptive experience. It's healthy, it's good, it's waking up, it's everybody waking up.

Yes, and not being afraid to use your body in a new way.

Getting off the ground is hard for some people, but when you're supported like that, it's great.

It's interesting to me because, at least in my experience, dancers who are highly trained sometimes have a harder time in aerial dance than others.

Yes, oh yes, I've found that too. I had a lot of problems with that. Sometimes, if dancers come from strict ballet or modern training, they just don't get the improvisation experience. They like technique. But improvisation frees up a lot of the technique of things. It's freeing and creative. Over the years, I came back to appreciating the importance of training in technical ways. I had fought it for so long and then I was coming back. I was glad I did that. And my work showed that in later years – the technique. So, I did appreciate it, and I used it, but I still had my own thing. I believe in improvisation in making aerial work.

Sometimes students don't necessarily know how to contribute in class. If they've never had experience with improvisation, they may not have a voice.

Well, that was it. [Students would say] "Tell me what to do. What do you mean play with this or play with that? Why would I do that?" I went through that with my improvisation teacher as well.

[When I was teaching] it was always a collaboration. I never came in knowing what I was going to do. I was like, "Okay improvise and let me watch and see what you're going to do." I even did this with myself. Improvise. I had a video [camera] that I was using, so I could video what I was doing and take it home and look at it. "Do I like that?" I like collaborating with myself and the video.

You developed the single point trapeze. Are there more opportunities in movement with that apparatus versus others?

Well, you know I didn't really have anything to compare it to at the time. When I started using the single point trapeze. I had the parallel ropes at one point as well. There was a freedom in it with the improvisation, and the swinging and the coming up and hooking around and flying. So, I liked that too. I felt a great sense of freedom with that. I think my students loved it too. The way I taught, I gave them the opportunity and the freedom to explore. And so, yeah, the single point trapeze of course changed things a lot because it would twist and turn and it would do everything that a dancer, a trained dancer, could do but it was freedom from gravity, using gravity. I mean, gravity is always there, and we knew that of course, and that served us. It wasn't completely without gravity, but we had gravity from above and gravity from below.

So, gravity was your partner?

Yeah, and the sense of freedom, being able to let the trapeze be a partner and a collaborator. You know, my partner, the trapeze! And it was certainly that, then the bungees, rope and harness. Rope and harness came later to me. I used the hoop in a lot of different ways as I developed, and rope and harness. I think it was the latter part of my work and I just said, "Oh well, this is fun, this is easy! It's easy to hang, it's easy to create." And then bungees that was another thing, that was free and that was exciting. And the freedom of using the bungee at a single point, Yeah, I used the bungee a lot.

Did you have a sense, when you were making this work, that you were the only one doing it, that you were the first?

Well, I mean I didn't even think of that because I was the only one and nobody else was paying any attention to me and they didn't consider it dance. "Oh, that's therapy, that's self-indulgent," [they'd say]. [There was] a lot of negativity. I mean I knew that Mary Martin had done Peter Pan, and Trisha Brown did things along the wall. That I heard about. I knew of these people but I didn't really see them doing what I was doing, but I was only informed by the photos. There was a Russian company that was kind of circus and dance. They did this beautiful piece and they had some trapezes above and they had a trampoline below, and they would dance, and then bounce themselves up to the trapezes and then come back down, and they used it all. That was like the first production I'd seen and I somehow didn't connect that with what I was doing. I was on the ground and I hadn't done a lot with trampoline. So they had the trampoline, which I loved, and I had done some trapeze already but I hadn't combined them yet.

I've been described as the mother of aerial dance, and only because I taught so many people. There was another woman who did anti-gravitational dance theatre. They did theatre and dance in the air. She was one of the first people to use aerial work. But they didn't credit her as "the mother". And I don't care. I don't really care if they call me grandmother or what. That's not what's important. What's important is what people are doing and what they are considering doing. It's a sense of freedom, basically. Flying is freedom. [Many, many years later] I went to Colorado where Nancy [Smith] had managed this grand festival. I was nervous. I was going to go do this *thing*. Teach what I'm doing! I went up there to do a workshop. So I was like, "Wow, this is nice. We really have a movement here. Other people are doing this! What an honor!" Nancy's festival [International Aerial Dance Festival] is going into the 17th year now. Every year [there are] new things, new apparatuses, and new dancers internationally. I can't say I invented it. I was a pioneer, that's what I was, and I had that single point trapeze and I had introduced the bungee, and maybe some others were doing the bungee as well, but no one from here. So, I might be more associated with the West coast.

Some aerial companies and schools are born out of circus and others' lineages are through dance.

Absolutely! People come and they want [to learn tricks]. It is hard to work for the people who have [only studied] circus, as well as the people who are extremely [trained in] ballet or modern. But it all fits a little easier now. We say the lines are blurred now. And they are. However, people clap after everything in circus. With dance it's not the same. I don't know if people did that with me, but I didn't like it if they did. That's the way [circus] sees things, and they are exquisite, and they have contributed a lot to the technical aspects of aerial.

Would you say the main difference between circus and aerial dance is intent? That dance has a communicative power?

Yeah, I do. I think that circus is there to make you go "Ah! Are they going to fall?" or "How big can it be? Boom! Look at us!" That's what excites people. My wife was into circus for kids. She started a whole program for kids that wasn't aerial dance, but circus. Some circus-oriented aerial is great. It's beautiful.

Can you talk to me a little bit about what your class was like when you were teaching?

Now that was my real art form. Again, I considered the whole scene, the whole person, and acknowledged people, so when people came in I really made a point to acknowledge everybody and get to know everybody and could sense what people needed. I had a sense of what I was doing and even though it was improvisation there was a way that I knew how to lead a group. I didn't stand in front of them and tell them what to do. I walked around and gave my instructions among them. I had them on a colorful, colorful mat. I really took great care to provide an environment they felt safe and comfortable. Not that I didn't demonstrate on the trapeze, sometimes I did. But mostly it was like giving instructions through words about how to explore. So, I would say, explore this, or see how it feels to you to explore this. I would start very low on the ground and work their way up in a safe and supportive way, and I cared a lot. I learned from Al Wunder. He was my mentor, and I really learned from him how to present things in such a way that they could take the material and do it their way, and that was important. Everybody got to do their own dance. I wanted to give them something to explore and experience on a deep physical-body sensation level. I would say, "What are you feeling in your body now? What are the sensations you are aware of in your body?" So, it's all about awareness, and I'm not sure everybody got what I was saying, but I knew that that was what was really important. And now, instead of awareness it's called mindfulness. The thing about that awareness was that it really took into consideration, not only what your body sensations were, but what you were feeling emotionally, what you were thinking. It's okay to think as long as you are aware and attentive to your thinking process. We need to be thinking. Imagination is part of your mind. Feldenkrais was my thing rather than Laban, and then it got to be Pilates. But I think Feldenkrais was the biggest awareness work [I studied] when I started developing my improvisation and my aerial work. My teaching was [modeled on] Feldenkrais'. And his teachers, though they may have been up in the front directing, didn't tell you what to do. It was all about exploring. The teachers gave so much room for the people to explore and experiment. How does this feel? To move just one little part of you, how does that feel? [The students say], "Oh, wow, I never thought of that before." So, that was what I really wanted to teach too, so when I taught, that was my way of teaching. Not giving directions so much but giving experiential projects.

Was there a point in class where the personal was shared or was it sort of always a private thing?

Oh no, I always had the sharing. "Get a partner now, or get two other people. Talk about how you're feeling now." And sometimes they didn't like that. It was personal. They weren't used to that, expressing themselves so intimately to somebody else, but it served everybody really well. And that was important. It was a wholeness. The whole is bigger than the sum of the parts. It was all about inclusion and that was feminism too. I was really into that. But it wasn't like a staunch *this is feminism*. I encouraged it, inclusion, being able to really be aware of somebody else, and acceptance of other people's work. Disabled people could come, transsexual people could come. My one regret was that I never had very many African-Americans. When I did the *Women Walking Tall Stilt Dancing*, that was inclusive, and that was probably the most "whole" thing I did politically, spiritually, feminine, body, mind, and spirit. It was big, all ages, all sizes. So, I was pleased to be able to include like that and I wish I had been able to do it more. But, my classes were accessible and that was important to me.

One of the things I love about modern dance is that the pioneers are women. It was originally a dance form made by women for women's bodies. And I feel like there is a similar thing going on in aerial. It seems to be predominantly women who are creating, performing and managing companies.

Yeah, no men with the companies that I know of. Well, maybe Robert Davidson [who is working in Seattle, WA]. He was my student. He's a beautiful dancer and choreographer and has done a lot of aerial work and done it beautifully, but in this area it seems to be mostly the women. [They have] different motivations, but they all just love aerial.

There is an entrepreneurial spirit.

Yes, I was about 10 years ahead of them. I started and then they came in. There was Krissy Keefer and Jo Kreiter and myself. Krissy Keefer is a force by herself. She does social-political work. She's a genius and she has these amazing shows, here and in other countries. She would [work] for the oppressed. But she started a thing called the *Revolutionary Nutcracker Sweetie* [premiered in 1987]. Jo Kreiter was on bungees. BANDALOOP was in the show. I got to know Amelia [Rudolph] and Jo through that. They are all very strong women. Joanna [Zaccho Dance Theatre] and her husband create beautiful things. I'm in love with him. Joanna is doing an aerial dance festival now. BANDALOOP will be performing in it, and Jo Kreiter will too. However, Krissy was the one that really put us out there to be seen. Especially me, I was first in her show but it became a sequential thing for about seven years in a glorious building. Krissy really put fire under a lot of us, and gave us a venue. She gave me many venues. She's an amazing artist, revolutionary, great revolutionary dancer. And Amelia, I don't really know what to say except for hanging in high places and dangling off of buildings is like, "Oh my gosh". You can't help but watch it and say *gasps*. We were all doing our own thing. Trying to raise the money and get people to dance with us. We didn't get together to discuss.

We just did our work. We had great influences. I love this community. We know each other and respect each other. We recognize what a trek it was to get up and do it. When you go that far out in space like BANDALOOP and Zaccho, it's exciting. It's exciting to look at the development and then Nancy [Smith] brought a lot of people together and that's where the international people are doing amazing work. Nancy is blending circus and aerial dance people [at the International Aerial Dance Festival in Boulder, CO.]

Where did your desire originate?

When I was going to grad school, I studied the history of dance. I wanted to be a pioneer like Martha [Graham]. Then [Alwin] Nikolais came along and I was introduced to his work and was able to attend a few workshops with him and Murray Lewis. Both of them were fabulous teachers. Murray had done a circus piece, and Nikolais really included the whole environment, like Merce Cunningham had. They could all see that it wasn't just the stage. It was bigger than that. It was cameras and lighting and music and everything. It was the entire theatre. I thought that Nikolais was it, and I sort of took off from there. When I came out here [CA] I met Al Wunder, my mentor, and Tandy Beal, an exquisite dancer, and other people that were with Nikolais. It influenced me a lot to see the whole picture. Merce Cunningham was like that too. Look at the whole picture. He had helium balloon pillows, so he did some aerial work.

What excites you now?

I'm writing a memoir. It's more like an autobiography. People ask me, "What's your book about . . . ?" It's about me! It is about the process I started with. When I was 12 years old someone asked me what I wanted to be when I grew up, I said I wanted to be a famous artist. I didn't say rich and famous. Should've said rich and famous! *laughs* I was writing about my struggles and overcoming this and overcoming that, as well as my triumphs. In case some artist wants to read about the process of how I created and how I taught, or how I overcame cancer and dealt with it in my art, about being an out lesbian. I didn't really present work that was based on that particularly, but I mostly worked with women in my creations, and I think that probably is because I am a lesbian. I wasn't really putting out that message necessarily, but I wasn't hiding it either. I came out pretty early. I can't dance anymore. I'm retired. I feel quite happy about it. I reflect on it as I am writing my book. It's called *Can You See Me Dancing?* because I felt like no one could see me for a long time. No one was watching. I couldn't understand why I was doing these amazing things and no one was watching. Gwen Jones was my accompanist through much of my work. She influenced me a lot. She wrote a song "Can you see me flying?". She knew my nightmare. So that's where I got the name for my book. I owe so much gratitude to her. She knew what I was doing and she did what she did in harmony with me. I've had a lot of really good people [in my life] and I finally feel like people have seen me flying. I now feel seen. I love to talk about aerial dance because it offers a sense of freedom for men and women. Children now too are doing it, and with such love. Why *not* offer it to the university?

skinner/kirk DANCE ENSEMBLE

Portland, OR

skinner/kirk DANCE ENSEMBLE *is a Portland-based dance company that has been guided since 1998 by the artistic vision of founders Eric Skinner and Daniel Kirk. For the Ensemble Skinner and Kirk develop original choreographic projects firmly rooted in the classical but informed by decades performing with modern and contemporary choreographers. skinner/kirk DANCE ENSEMBLE's work serves to expand the range of aesthetic experiences for company dancers, collaborating artists, and audience members throughout the region. Since its founding, s/kDE has self-produced six full evenings of original dance, collaborating with musicians, filmmakers, composers, fashion designers, sculptors and performance artists. The company has been presented multiple times in Portland by* BodyVox, *and appeared in* White Bird's *2009 Uncaged Series where they premiered a new commissioned work.* skinner/kirk DANCE ENSEMBLE *has received support for the creation of new work from* Regional Arts and Culture Council *(RACC) in 2002, and the Bessie* Schonberg Choreographic Mentorship Residency *at* The Yard *in 2014. The company was recognized by the* IRS *as a 501© (3) nonprofit organization in 2013.*

What is your definition of aerial dance?

Simply, we see aerial dance as movement off the ground. That can be the more traditional apparatus, like trapeze, ropes, silks, bungees, etc., or structures suspended above the floor, giving dancers a different challenge and dimension.

What sort of background do your dancers come from? How do they transition to aerial?

For the most part, our dancers come from a strong dance background with an emphasis on ballet training. When we first started working with aerial, and developing our technique and vocabulary, we were collaborating with more modern dancers. It was a great blend of backgrounds to experiment and create what would become our aerial language. As we have gone on to create and set newer works, we have gravitated toward the line and quality of movement in ballet-trained dancers. One of the challenges with using dancers in our aerial work is the lack of upper body strength. We have to build in a period of conditioning and adjustment for the dancers to be able to translate their artistry from the ground to aerial.

Can you speak to the communicative powers of aerial dance?

Much of our choreographic work in general is abstract, but always evocative of a mood, or theme. We feel audiences are transformed by watching aerial. It has the ability to transport, and create the experience of another world, one not bound to the earth. In an instance where we used it in a narrative story, we used slings to create the experience of drowning. The feeling portrayed could never have been as evocative and visceral had it been choreographed with traditional contemporary movement.

How do you feel about content in aerial performance? How do you explore expressionism/ storytelling/communication in aerial dance?

We are in agreement that aerial movement is another form of dance that can either be explored on its own, or in concert with other forms of dance. Part of communicating a story is to make the movement human and relatable. While most people would not be able to relate to weightlessness, and being air-bound, we think that on its own, it does not have the same potential for communication as other, earth-bound movement.

Do you feel a strong improvisational education is necessary for aerial?

Especially in the creative process, strong improvisational skills are definitely important. One aspect of the types of apparatus we use, is that the ropes, bungee, slings, etc. have a bit of a mind of their own. If you try to resist, or fight the apparatus you will miss the true experience of it. So having the freedom of comfort with improvising lets you adapt to the nuances of the ropes.

What role does fear play?

Fear should not be a factor in aerial work. If you are harboring fears of the work, then you are not available to embody it and dance. Risk is a better sensation to explore in this context. Pushing the level of where you are comfortable, both physically and artistically, is where the experience will really be rewarding for the performers and the viewers.

What does a typical class look like for the dancers?

We have created a syllabus for our movement, somewhat codifying the technique, and approach classes and workshops with a structured template. Like a traditional dance class, there is a warm up period, then technical exercises, followed by exploration and discovery. We understand that for beginners, muscle burn out and dizziness are imminent factors, so pacing is important. As the level of experience increases, the more we can push the dancers to increase skill, conditioning and artistry.

Do you feel that rehearsing for aerial is enough to prepare you for aerial? Or do you advocate a plan for optimal conditioning?

Depending on the amount of aerial training the dancer is engaged with on a weekly basis, we would advocate cross conditioning. Strength training, yoga, endurance training, dance classes can all enhance the ability to perform aerial movement. Like any dance form, rising above the technical and physical challenges is when it really becomes artistic. Though if you're really immersed in your aerial training, it is an amazing, full body workout, and could definitely be enough to prepare you for further work and performance.

What do your dancers need to bring to the table?

Whether we are working in aerial, or traditional dance styles, we choose to work with dancers who have an open mind, a collaborative spirit, and a sense of creativity. We hope that a dancer will jump in, discover vocabulary on their own, bring context to movement and feel a connection to the work.

How does aerial contribute to the modern dance canon?

We see aerial as a discrete genre in the modern dance canon. While cross genre skills always bring new elements to any work, we're not sure how aerial will affect other forms of modern dance. We believe that aerial dance is a unique genre on its own, and even within that, has so many variations to it. We see so many companies that approach aerial from so many different aspects, not always dance. Some are more inclined to the circus arts, some from a more athletic vision, so it would be hard to say that it is a reframing of traditional dance, it can be so separate from that.

Talk about the rigors of aerial from an equipment standpoint. Are your harnesses/ equipment custom made?

We source our ropes, generally using static climbing rope. For trapezes and slings and other harness type of gear, we build our own. We replace the wood on the trapezes regularly for safety, inspect padding and webbing, knots and rigging. When on tour, each rigging process is a little unique, so being adaptable and knowledgeable is important, as is having a good supply of gear available.

What is your approach to teaching?

We did create a technique organically with no formal training. At the time we were experimenting and creating our first works, around 1996/97, there was no known network for artists experimenting in this genre, yet it was happening all over. An important dance presenter in Boston noted this phenomenon, and sought out aerial dance makers from around the world and brought us together for a festival in Boston designed to showcase the work, and create discussion between artists to share inspirations, resources and technique. It was an amazing experience for so many of us early creators, and so interesting to see how differently everyone had approached the genre. One thing we really noticed at the festival was how most of the groups approached it with a very athletic take. Very few had really layered on the sense of theater that elevated it from an inventive use of aerial apparatus to artistic expression through movement that was airborne. Our previous work in professional dance companies had informed the theatrical aspects of our early aerial work, and it has motivated our intent since.

Is your work characteristically architectural or conceptual?

Most of our aerial work on trapeze is approached from an architectural standpoint. Shape and line are important aspects of our work. Our pieces often take on subtext through the creative process, we set out to create a mood, or build on a theme, and then we allow it to take on meaning through the process. Our soundscapes, and lighting design are crafted to support those themes, and are often layered on after the piece begins to take shape.

Do you have a mentor?

We can't really say that we had a strong mentor in developing our technique. Robert Davidson was doing similar work in Seattle at that time and that was definitely an inspiration, but our informative experimentation was very insulated, and came from a very organic, home-grown place.

Do you feel pressure to try to "fit" aerial into the dance continuum?

Almost 20 years into creating aerial movement, and performing it around the world, we believe that aerial dance is already seen as a legitimate form of movement that fits snugly amidst many other genres.

What advice would you give aspiring college students who want to be aerial dancers?

Initially, our advice would be to jump in and experiment, take classes if available, get online and research who out there is creating work that inspires or interests you and follow the impulse. Eventually, it would be important to look deeper and make sure you're in the best hands possible to push you in the direction you seek. And don't be afraid to acknowledge that the best hands may be your own. In our case, going into a studio for six to ten hours a week and experimenting over the course of a year and a half to discover and create our own unique voice was extremely fulfilling.

Sharon Witting, Elevate Arts
Takoma Park, MD

Elevate Arts *is an aerial arts company delivering high impact performance and high caliber instruction for audiences of all ages and abilities in Washington DC, Maryland, and Virginia. Founded and directed by Sharon Witting,* Elevate Arts *is available for public performances, corporate events, group classes, artistic residencies, team-building workshops, private lessons, and creative collaboration. Classically trained in ballet and modern dance, Sharon began flying at the San Francisco School of Circus Arts in 1999, was a founding member of* Air Dance Bernasconi, *and continues her training at the* New England Center for Circus Arts. *She is co-founder of the award-winning* Arachne Aerial Arts, *DC's first aerial arts company that performed in theaters, museums, galleries, and festivals for more than a decade. She holds a BA in Anthropology from Washington & Lee University and an MAT in Museum Education from George Washington University.*

What sort of background do your dancers come from? Do you see any issues when transitioning from other forms to aerial?

My students range from beginners to professionals. While some movement training is helpful for drawing inspiration, understanding feedback, applying corrections, and communicating physio/expressive qualities, I don't believe that one type of training is more useful than another. Most of my professional students draw on prior training in classical dance, contact improv, yoga, and gymnastics, but some have little dance training at all. Because my own background is classical dance, that is the language I speak best, but each movement style has important applications to aerial dance.

Can you speak to the communicative powers of aerial dance?

I believe that metaphors are very strong in aerial dance. Every human being has dreamed of flight at one time or another, and the quest for that freedom provides commonality among choreographers, performers, and audiences. Aerial apparatus are more than props, they are dance partners that can transport not only the performers, but also the viewers who are drawn into the performance space. I've seen people sway in their chairs to the rhythm of the piece, I've heard them weep from memories unearthed during performances. These are powerful, visceral responses that are rare in life, and very special in performance.

Do you feel a strong improvisational education is necessary for aerial?

Absolutely. Aerial apparatus do not behave predictably at all times. Performance conditions vary widely, partners get sick or injured, and it is difficult to recreate a performance space in the studio. Even the tightest choreographed dance can shift with the wind, literally, when performing outdoors. Every artist, whether performer, or choreographer, must be skilled at adapting to unintended challenges and opportunities. These improvised moments, when the artist must go off script, are often the most interesting and inspired in my opinion. Staying present in the moment is essential to compelling live performance of any kind. With aerial dance, the stakes are higher, literally, as unplanned events can have safety implications. For artists without improvisational training, the best form of education is experience.

In what ways do your dancers contribute?

Beyond the strength, stamina, flexibility, and technique required to communicate effectively and safely in the air, an aerial dancer must have humility to know what s/he doesn't know, respect for physical and emotional boundaries, adaptability in challenging performance situations, commitment to hard work and self improvement, and last but not least, confidence in self advocacy, especially if a situation feels unsafe. I encourage dancers to seek training from as many safe coaches as they can, because they will draw on these experiences when working with others and creating their own choreography.

What is your approach to teaching? Do you have a structured class?

As a classical dancer, I am fairly rigorous about technique. However, the loveliest technique void of expression doesn't speak to me as an artist or an audience member. I work hard with students to develop their artistic voices and the nuances of self-expression. I believe that every dancer, every performer, is also a choreographer with a story to tell. Not all dancers are comfortable taking on that role, preferring to remain anonymous in someone else's drama. We are all agents of our own drama, and drama is what compels us. Within each lesson, I try to balance the ingredients of successful performance in my mind: technique, expression, invention, and drama.

Safety Test

Figure A.01 Safety is paramount
Credit: © Washington and Lee University

SAFETY TEST

When performing aerial what are the two most important safety considerations?

_____

_____

_____

What is the biggest problem with equipment?

_____

_____

_____

When you are prepared to go on the wall, what do you say to your partner so that they go over your equipment?

_____

_____

_____

What are the basic harness checkpoints for safety?

_____

_____

_____

Specifically requesting a check on the closure of the carabiner is called what?

_____

_____

_____

Where should the waist belt of your harness sit?

_____

_____

_____

SAFETY TEST – *continued*

What is a "cross loaded" carabiner?

_____

_____

_____

What is the carabiner safety phrase?

_____

_____

_____

How do you tell if a belt is double backed?

_____

_____

_____

What are the parts of the harness? Where are they located?

_____

_____

_____

What is the equipment that allows you to "climb" up the rope called?

_____

_____

_____

What is the procedure for "climbing" the rope? Describe each step.

_____

_____

_____

SAFETY TEST – *continued*

What is the equipment set up between the rig point and the harness at the beginning of a climb?

_____

_____

_____

What is the name of the equipment that allows you to lower yourself?

_____

_____

_____

What is the procedure coming off the wall? Describe each step.

_____

_____

_____

What is the appropriate attire for aerial dance?

_____

_____

_____

Who should be in the room at all times when rehearsing on the wall?

_____

_____

_____

 This safety test is also available on the companion website, www.routledge/cw/davies

APPENDIX B

Equipment Vocabulary

Figure B.01 Equipment fluency is an essential skill for all aerialists

Credit: © Washington and Lee University 2016

Ascender: a piece of climbing equipment used to "climb" a rope. Can be made of aluminum or stainless steel and usually has a plastic handgrip. The ascender has a molded semi circular area at the top for the rope to slide into. Next to this area is a locking mechanism which opens to insert the rope and locks closed to grip the rope. An ascender can slide up the rope but cannot slide down.

Belay loop: one of the loops on a climbing harness. This loop is in the front, middle portion of the harness, near the belly button and is bar tacked for maximum safety. This is the main clip-in point for the carabiner. Harnesses can have a single belay loop or they can also have clip-in points on the sides, back and at the center of the back of the chest harness. Be sure not to confuse clip-in points with gear loops. It can mean the difference between life and death. Belay loops can be fabric or metal depending on the type of harness.

Carabiner: pear, triangular, oval or D shaped aluminum or stainless steel mechanism used to connect equipment to equipment or people to equipment. Contains a gate which presses open to insert a piece of equipment. The gate either has a self-locking mechanism or screws down manually.

Climbing rope: specially constructed rope that can be either static or dynamic. Dynamic rope stretches a bit and static does not. In a circumstance involving a long, hard fall, dynamic rope can make an arrest less painful because the rope has a bit of stretch. For aerial dance, I always use static rope and I do not want any sort of stretching. Static rope contains a core composed of individual braided strands. A braided sheath covers the individual strands and protects them from wear and tear and the elements. The diameter of a climbing rope can vary from approximately 8.5mm to 16mm.

Double backed: a term used to define a belt buckle that is in safety mode. That is, a belt, leg, shoulder or riser that is threaded through the buckle and then the end of which is then threaded back through the start of the buckle. When double backed properly, the buckle looks like a "C". When a buckle is not double backed it looks like an "O". Many harnesses have permanently double backed elements to improve safety.

Foot loop: although we use this term in class, the item used is actually called a sling. This is a flat strand of polyethylene or nylon that is very strong, and thin and is sewn into a loop with heavy duty bar tacks insuring that the rope cannot come apart. Widths can vary from 12–18mm and lengths from 30–240 mm.

Gacflex: product name for a spanset. This particular spanset is a continuous loop and has a core of metal wires (galvanixed aircraft cable) surrounded by a polyester sheath. Gacflex comes in various sizes to carry varying loads.

Gear loop: fabric loops attached usually to the back and sides of a harness. They are present to hold equipment for climbing but rarely used in aerial dance. We tend to loop our extra rope through them in class. They are not designed to carry the weight of a person. Clipping into a gear loop can result in injury or death.

Grigri: product name for a descender. A piece of equipment used for both maintaining position on a rope and assisted braking when descending a rope. Can be either stainless steel or aluminum. Front plate slides open for rope insertion. Once closed and attached to a carabiner, the rope slides through the grigri when climbing and the cam pinches shut to lock your position on the rope and prevent falling. Handle opens and with pressure, allows for gradual release down the rope.

Harness: a fabric frame for the pelvis or pelvis/chest for use in carrying the body into the air via a rope or other means. Varying harnesses can offer padding in waist and/or legs and shoulders and most are equipped with adjustable leg loops, waist band, shoulder and/or chest loops and sometimes adjustable risers. Some models have pre-threaded, double backed waist belt, leg loops, shoulder straps, chest strap and risers. Geer loops and belay loop circle the waist. Most models come in XS, S, M, L, XL.

Leg loops: fabric loops on the bottom of the harness that are designed to fit around the thighs. Leg loops are sometimes attached to the waist band via risers in the back and tie in loops and belay loop in the front. Some leg loops are padded for comfort and most are adjustable to fit varying body sizes.

Swivel: metal piece of equipment, either stainless steel or aluminum, that prevents the rope from twisting as a person spins. Consists of two pieces, each generally semi circular or triangular, joined at the center and containing ball bearings that create a smooth spinning motion. Swivel is generally placed at the top of the rig and connected to the rope via a carabiner through the top and bottom openings.

Waist belt: the portion of the harness that encircles the waist and should sit above the hip bones. Contains a metal buckle that is either pre-threaded or permanently double backed but can be as simple as a long fabric piece that gets threaded through the metal buckle and hand double backed. Waist belt can have varying degrees of padding and size is a determining factor in the overall size of the harness.

 Reference Online Information B.1. *Equipment Vocabulary*

Terminology

COMMONLY USED TERMS

Alignment for aerial is very important. Because you spend most of your time either resisting or giving in to gravity, it sort of feels like dancing with a ten pound weight that can shift position and speed at any given moment. For this reason, among others, being properly aligned means safety for the dancer. Alignment must also go hand in hand with lengthening. For example, to crunch up your abdominals in a little ball might mean that you are able to plank but it probably also means that your shoulders, neck and head are out of

Figure C.1 Center floor rope and harness duet
Credit: © Washington and Lee University 2011

alignment and therefore prone to injury. Instead of using the word "contraction", I tend to say "press your belly button to your spine" or "push your abs into your back". I feel that this type of imagery carries with it an inherent lengthening. It helps the dancer to know which muscles to engage but also the way in which they are engaging. For new aerialists and beginning students, I usually take time during the floor warm up to palpate the abdominal muscles and, using the floor as a point of reference, have them press into the floor and feel the floor through their back. I've used, with much success, a sphygmomanometer for this same purpose. I place a deflated sphygmomanometer cuff under their lumbar then inflate it to a pressure of 20 millimeters, and ask the student to press their abdominals back into their spine and watch the dial raise. I instruct them to try to push the number higher and then hold it (but keep breathing and encouraging them to allow their stomach to rise and fall with their breath). Then after 20–30 seconds they release and come back to a rest. In this way, the students *feel* what engaging their abdominals means. (This can also be used as a gentle way to gain strength in their abdominals and lower back.) I also work palpating the bones and muscles that contribute to proper alignment. We work and talk through what their *center line* is – center of the skull, sternum, abdominals and public bone. (Many times the knees and ankles are part of the line as well.) Alignment's partner is elongation. The bones must be in their proper place and the dancer must be reaching away and elongating, in the appropriate way, from the torso.

Figure C.2 Proper alignment in plank
Credit: © Washington and Lee University 2016

When I talk about the *L position*, I am referring to the shape of the body. In an L position, the dancer is in a sitting position facing the wall, with their legs out straight against the wall. This position begins many of the warm up exercises. It gives the dancer a chance to warm up her/his body without placing stress too soon on the abdominals. In an L position, the dancer is sitting tall in the harness. The top of their head is reaching up to the ceiling. The back is elongated and the vertebra are stacked one on top of the other. Be careful about leaning back into the harness (this happens when dancers get tired and it throws the torso out of alignment) and also watch to be sure the lumbar is not arched. The abdominals should be pressing backwards against the spinal column. The pelvis is sitting directly below the shoulder girdle. The head of the femur is in line with the knees and ankles, as the legs stretch out directly parallel from the pelvis to the wall. Be sure that the head is in alignment by checking that the dancer's face is parallel to the wall and the back of their neck is long.

The *plank position* is a much more intense position than the L. This is because the body is parallel to the ground and, in order to stay that way, the abdominals, the muscles of the lower back and a host of other muscles must be activated. In the plank position, the feet are flexed and against the wall and are in alignment with the legs, pelvis, spine, and top of the head. In order to correctly execute this position, the abdominals must be contracted and the pelvis must be pushing back against the harness. The lower back muscles are engaged and work with the abdominals supporting the horizontal position. The upper abdominals are

Figure C.3 L position
Credit: © Washington and Lee University 2016

engaged. I use imagery of being zipped closed from pubic bone to sternum. One frequent difficulty for students in this position is the shoulder girdle. Students tend to be weak in their upper abdominals (and heads are heavy!) and drop their shoulders downward, away from the torso. When this happens the neck becomes disengaged and the head misaligns. This accounts for a lot of muscular neck soreness and pain the next day. This is a very intense position and, I've learned from experience, that using it too often with beginners fatigues the students to the point of exhaustion. Using it prudently will gradually, over time, build up the students' strength.

Figure C.4 Plank position
Credit: © Washington and Lee University 2016

The *T position* is used when the dancer faces the side. Typically, due to the orientation of the harness, if the dancer is in L or plank, the chest is facing the wall or ceiling, respectively. But when movements like somersaults occur, the dancer begins on her side. The position is complex anatomically because you must engage your abdominals and lower back muscles to keep you in a plank but because of the way you are hanging, gravitational force is pulling you down to one side. Internal obliques are used to help keep you erect, and the back and shoulder girdle to help maintain equilibrium. This position can be especially problematic for dancers who have disproportionately long legs or long torso. It causes them to pitch one way or the other. In some cases, the type of harness that the dancer wears can help. Harnesses that are reinforced in the pelvis with lots of padding and thick belts may be of help to dancers with extra long torsos. Similarly, harnesses with thinner straps, less padding and generally lighter weight may help aerialists with short torsos. The T position is generally arrived at through the L and then the plank. The dancer should focus on individual aspects of a correct T position as he moves through the other positions and into it. For example, the dancer focuses on elongating the spine, neck and head as she sits in the L position. Then, as she moves through L to plank, she focuses on engaging the abdominals, lower back, upper back and shoulders. Finally, as the body turns over to the side into a T, all of the above musculature is still working, though somewhat differently with the shift of the body, and the obliques engage along with correct shoulder, neck and head alignment, and proper leg positioning. This gradual release into T, through other positions, aids in thoughtful movement to achieve ideal alignment. In order for this position to be completed accurately, the harness must be shifted to the side. The carabiner and grigri will shift to one hip. If there is excessive room between the dancer and her harness, the aerialist needs to come down off of the wall and tighten the waist belt of the harness. The leg loops may seem to shift when you turn on your side, especially if there are elastic risers in the back. If you feel confined by the leg loops, don't loosen them. The leg loops being tight is integral to the safety of the dancer. Just loosen the riser in the back. This will allow a little more length between the waist belt and the leg loops. In the T position, the weight of the head is more noticeable then in other positions. Be aware that when flipping and somersaulting, more often than not, the head and shoulders

Figure C.5 T position
Credit: © Washington and Lee University 2016

will dip down. This can lead to misjudging the distance the dancer needs to be away from the wall, leading to contact between the wall and the dancer's helmet. Obviously we want to avoid that. In the early stages of working in the T position, be aware that weakness in the upper body is a concern and take steps to spot spinning into and away from the wall until the student develops both an understanding of the force and balance necessary for spins and flips and the musculature necessary to perform it.

Adding arms to the exercises adds to the difficulty level muscularly and, when moving through space, adds resistance and centrifugal forces. Because my training is in Horton technique (and because I love the clean lines) my arm positions are loosely based on that technique. In an exercise with no arms mentioned or if I indicate *first position* arms, this means the arms are straight down at the sides. The shoulder girdle is activated and energy flows down through the shoulders and out the fingertips. There is a downward, reaching force emanating from the arms, wrists, hands, and fingers that is in opposition to the upward reach from the spine through the top of the head. I like the arms to be touching the sides of the harness and not to fly away as the dancer moves from position to position. (That type of arm work is incorporated during phase or choreographic work.) For any work done in *second position*, arms are out to the sides of the body. They are not directly straight out from the shoulders but angled slightly forward so that, when looking directly ahead, you can see them in your peripheral vision. They are straight and reaching long and away from the torso. I tell my students to imagine they are holding a bucket of water over each wrist. This image aids in keeping energy in the arms. They should be engaged, pressing up and reaching long. Anything performed in *fifth position* (I don't tend to use much third or fourth position with beginning level students although certainly any of these exercises can use those positions as well) is accomplished with arms straight up at my ears. In this position, you press your shoulders down while at the same time reaching your arms up to the ceiling and touching your ears. Energy flows up through your arms and they stretch long and away from your body. Using these arms while in plank adds quite a bit of weight to the body, which is already facing much downward force from the horizontal position. I use these arms with advanced or very strong dancers. It's important to build the strength of the dancers up slowly, teaching correct alignment and posture throughout the process. If you jump to advanced work right away not only can you injure your student but you risk them burning out after the first 15 minutes of class. Aerial works the body in ways that typical dancers and athletes aren't generally prepared for. It's a balancing act, not only to care for the well being and health of the students, but also to push them enough so they grow but not so much that they burn out. You want them present for the long haul so it's important to take baby steps. The technique grows as the dancer grows.

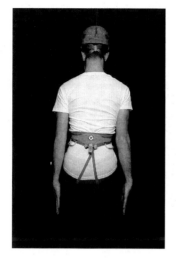

Figure C.06

Arm alignment in first position

Credit: © Washington and Lee
University 2016

Figure C.07

Arm alignment in second position

Credit: © Washington and Lee University 2016

Figure C.08

Arm alignment in fifth position

Credit: © Washington and Lee
University 2016

TERMS THAT CAN BE CONFUSING

I tend to default to either dance or gymnastic terms when describing movement. This is partially due to my education and training and partially because the general population has some sort of understanding of these terms which can help to provide an easy avenue towards understanding a complex mix of body position, orientation, force, and time. Sometimes, though, these terms can become complex when only small details characterize their differences. Other times the terms are so general that they've lost meaning and are open to interpretation. In an effort to clarify what might be confusing, here are a few examples.

Turn and Spin

For our purposes, I've delineated a difference between a *turn* and a *spin*. I do this because the vertical space is more than simply a surface. It can be used as our floor when we are in a plank, or as a parallel surface when we are in an L position. It's our springboard and our landing space. It can easily get confusing, spatially, when speaking about aerial movement, so specificity of terminology becomes very important. The path of an aerial turn, in traditional dance terms, would be considered one full turn. That is, the body moving from one facing, rotating and finishing at the same facing. A 360 degree path. Similarly, an aerial turn translates to pushing away from the wall while turning your back to the wall and returning to the wall just after your feet round the corner of the turn. If you imagine the wall as a straight line and you look down upon it from a birds eye view, in aerial dance you've pushed off from

Figure C.09 Turn
Credit: courtesy of Emma Davies-Mansfield

Figure C.10: Spin
Credit: courtesy of Emma Davies-Mansfield

the wall, traveled away in an arc and come back to rest. In a turn, you face the wall at the start and at the end but you never turn all the way around the rope that is holding you. A spin makes a complete circle around the rope. When you spin, you push off from the wall and make a complete turn before your feet hit the wall again. One simple way to understand this is to think about the person in relationship to the rig point of the rope. If the student rotates half way around the rig point, they've completed a turn. If they completely circle around the rope that is supporting them, they've spun. In a spin, the body begins facing the wall, you push off and your back faces the wall, then your front faces the wall as you are swinging, and then your back again before you land once more, in the starting position. In traditional terms, a spin would equate to two sequential turns. Both of these terms assume that your head is up and your feet are down. When we turn the body sideways, parallel to the ground we move into somersault, walkover and flip territory.

Ball Turn and Somersault

The concept that separates these terms is orientation. A *ball turn* happens when you are contracted into a ball position with your body in the correct up to down orientation in the frontal plane (as if you were standing on the ground). A *somersault* is basically the same body position except that the entire person is oriented in the transverse plane (perpendicular to a person standing on the ground). For a ball turn, a dancer goes from L to a contracted ball position. For a somersault the person goes from L position to plank to T position, then contracts into a ball.

Invert

This just means upside down. I use it with an *inverted* torso and with an inverted arabesque and turning inverted arabesque. The head is oriented towards the floor and the legs towards the ceiling.

Walkover and Flip

The difference between a *walkover* and a *flip* are the position of the legs and pelvis. In the walkover the legs are scissored with one in front and the other behind. The leading leg lands on the wall first followed by the other. The pelvis is flexible and extends and contracts based on the position of the legs. A flip is performed with legs together. Generally the pelvis is in alignment with the legs and the torso. The pelvis and legs move as one entity. Both the walkover and the flip can be performed with or without arms landing on the wall as the head passes.

Supported Flip and Flip (and Supported Walkover and Walkover)

Any *supported* exercise means that one arm is holding onto the rope. This is an option for beginners who have undeveloped musculature. By grasping the rope, you take (some) of the pressure off of your muscles so that you can perform a movement with proper alignment even if you haven't the strength to do so. (One must not pull the shoulders/head up with the arm that is holding the rope. This throws the body out of alignment as well.) Supported movements are meant to be a temporary help and forgone when proper strength is reached.

Cartwheel and Starfish

The difference between these exercises is its spatial design. Both require the body to be in an "X" position with arms and legs open at 45 degree angle from the torso. The body is flat using the back of the head, sternum, abdominals, pubic bones, knees, and ankles as alignment markers. A starfish pushes away from the wall in a straight line with the body held in this position and lands again on the feet. A cartwheel maintains the same position but moves along with wall swinging left to right in a circular motion. (A cartwheel can also be stationary.)

Turning Plank and Cartwheel

Muscularly these two movements are quite similar. The differences are based on effort/force and small elements of alignment. The *plank* requires a flat body where head, sternum, abdominals and pubic bone are aligned and the core is working to keep the shoulders and pelvis stabilized. The plank's legs are together and arms are at the sides (in first position). As you push off with your feet, your arms raise to either side of your head so that you can land on your hands as you finish the 180 degree turn. Your body revolves as a plank. There is a pause upon landing. You then bend your elbows and push off the wall, landing back on your feet to either go backwards repeating the prior 180 degree turn or forwards to complete the 360. The *cartwheel* has similar muscular demands but the position of the legs is at 45 degree angles from the body and the arms are overhead, 45 degrees from the skull. Instead of landing with both arms and then both legs, the cartwheel lands one arm at a time and then one leg at a time, creating a circular motion that is parallel to the ground. With the cartwheel there is a sustained effort as opposed to the turning plank where the effort is great, followed by a sustained pause followed by another effort to return to position. *Turning planks* are generally performed from a stable position whereas cartwheels occur in place or moving through space.

Turning T and Flip

The differences between a *turning T* and a *flip* are similar to those of the turning plank and cartwheel. Effort and force are different as one moves through space while the other is stationary but the general musculature is the same. The turning T moves from the aligned T position via a deep plié with enough force to complete a 180 degree semi circle landing on the hands. From there, following a pause, the elbows bend with a similar deep force and push the body back to where it originated either via a backwards motion, covering the same 180 degrees that brought you there, or forwards, completing the 360 degree circle. The turning T is comprised of brief spurts of excessive force followed by balance. A flip covers much of the same movement and shape qualities, but does not stop at the hands and continues in a 360 degree circle. A flip can be performed from a stationary position or traveling through space. Because a flip does not stop midway, it doesn't require advanced balancing skills. Similarly it's not as difficult muscularly because the force of the turn doesn't have to be arrested and held prior to engaging the force again.

BIOGRAPHY

Jenefer Davies is the Associate Professor of Dance at Washington and Lee University and Artistic Director of the W&L Repertory Dance Company. She received an MFA in Choreography and Performance from The George Washington University, and a MALS in Dance from Hollins University. Her choreography has been commissioned by dance, opera and theatre companies and has toured to Spain, Greece, Scotland, and throughout the United States. Davies founded the contemporary modern dance company, Progeny Dance, which has performed at Green Space and Dixon Place in Manhattan, and annually at The Center for Performance Research in Brooklyn, among others. Her work has been supported by the Virginia Commission for the Arts; Washington and Lee University's Lenfest Grants, Johnson Fund, and Glenn Grants; the Treakle Foundation; and an Associated Colleges of the South Mellon grant. She created one of the first academic programs in aerial dance in the country and her aerial dancers have performed at the Ailey Citigroup Theatre in NYC, at the Corcoran Gallery of Art in Washington DC, and from the rooftops of buildings on the Washington & Lee campus. Davies has been published in the International Planetarian Magazine, ICHPER-SD World Congress on Dance, the Nu Delta Alpha Journal and the Athens (Greece) Institute for Research in the Arts Consortium. She serves on the Editorial and Reviewer's Board of the Athens Journal of Humanities and Arts and has reviewed dance proposals for Oxford University Press.

Credit: © Washington and Lee University 2009

Index

 Taylor & Francis eBooks

Helping you to choose the right eBooks for your Library

Add Routledge titles to your library's digital collection today. Taylor and Francis ebooks contains over 50,000 titles in the Humanities, Social Sciences, Behavioural Sciences, Built Environment and Law.

Choose from a range of subject packages or create your own!

Benefits for you
>> Free MARC records
>> COUNTER-compliant usage statistics
>> Flexible purchase and pricing options
>> All titles DRM-free.

Benefits for your user
>> Off-site, anytime access via Athens or referring URL
>> Print or copy pages or chapters
>> Full content search
>> Bookmark, highlight and annotate text
>> Access to thousands of pages of quality research at the click of a button.

 REQUEST YOUR **FREE** INSTITUTIONAL TRIAL TODAY

Free Trials Available
We offer free trials to qualifying academic, corporate and government customers.

eCollections – Choose from over 30 subject eCollections, including:

Archaeology	Language Learning
Architecture	Law
Asian Studies	Literature
Business & Management	Media & Communication
Classical Studies	Middle East Studies
Construction	Music
Creative & Media Arts	Philosophy
Criminology & Criminal Justice	Planning
Economics	Politics
Education	Psychology & Mental Health
Energy	Religion
Engineering	Security
English Language & Linguistics	Social Work
Environment & Sustainability	Sociology
Geography	Sport
Health Studies	Theatre & Performance
History	Tourism, Hospitality & Events

For more information, pricing enquiries or to order a free trial, please contact your local sales team:
www.tandfebooks.com/page/sales

 Routledge
Taylor & Francis Group

The home of Routledge books

www.tandfebooks.com